Mary Anne's Makeover

Mary Anne's Makeover
Ann M. Martin

AN
APPLE
PAPERBACK

SCHOLASTIC INC.
New York Toronto London Auckland Sydney

Cover art by Hodges Solileau

No part of this publication may be reproduced in whole or in part, or stored in a retrieval system, or transmitted in any form or by any means, electronic, mechanical, photocopying, recording, or otherwise, without written permission of the publisher. For information regarding permission, write to Scholastic Inc., 730 Broadway, New York, NY 10003.

ISBN 0-590-45662-8

12 11 10 9 8 7 6 5 4 3 2 1   3 4 5 6 7 8/9

Printed in the U.S.A.   40

First Scholastic printing, January 1993

The author gratefully acknowledges
Peter Lerangis
for his help in
preparing this manuscript.

Mary Anne's Makeover

CHAPTER 1

"I found a flummp caterpillar!" Carolyn Arnold shouted from the basement.

Well, at least that was what it sounded like. It was hard to tell, because her twin sister Marilyn was practicing the piano loudly in the living room.

I was in the kitchen. I should say I'd been *banished* to the kitchen by my two eight-year-old baby-sitting charges. Marilyn, the musician, needed to practice. Carolyn, the science whiz, was working away on some mysterious project. Me? I'd started my math homework, but a flummp caterpillar sounded much more interesting. So I called out, "You found a what?" When I got no answer, I repeated, "You found a *what*?"

Carolyn came rushing into the kitchen. "Mary *Aaaanne*," she said with exasperation, "you know I can't hear you when Marilyn's playing."

I bit my lip. Normally I would have reminded her that she'd been calling *me*, but I didn't. You see, I had just made a New Year's resolution: to be the best person I could be, in all possible ways. (Okay, I admit I may have gone overboard with that resolution, but at least I could try.) And that meant being the best possible baby-sitter, along with everything else.

"Well, I'm glad you're here now," I said with kindness and patience. "Now, what did you say you found?"

"A flux capacitator!" Carolyn replied, holding up a magnifying glass with the lens missing.

"Uh-huh," I said. "What's that?"

Carolyn rolled her eyes. Then she leaned over and lowered her voice to a whisper. "Didn't you see *Back to the Future*? The flux capacitator is the secret to . . . you know . . ." She gestured, as if I were supposed to know what she meant.

"What, time travel?" I asked.

"Sshhhh!" Carolyn shot back. Then she whispered, "Yes!"

"Um, why are we whispering?" I asked.

"Because," Carolyn explained, "if anyone finds out about this, they'll try to steal my idea. I want to be totally finished with it before I let people use it."

2

As she scampered across the kitchen toward the basement door, I asked, "Use *what*, Carolyn?"

She pulled the door open, looked over her shoulder with a big smile, and said, "My time machine!"

Before I could reply, she was down the stairs.

The only sound left was Marilyn's song. She was playing this dainty classical piece that made me think of people with powdered faces dancing around in wigs and dresses with big bustles.

So there I was, with the ancient past in the Arnolds' living room and the future downstairs in the Arnolds' basement. I felt like some kind of midpoint on a time line. A big dot that says "You are here." And "here" was the Arnolds' kitchen on a cold, dreary Wednesday afternoon in January.

"You," of course, is me, Mary Anne Spier. And I don't mean to sound like I was miserable that afternoon or anything. I really love baby-sitting. In fact, as a Baby-sitters Club member, I consider it one of the most important things in my life (more about the BSC later). What are the other important things in my life? My family, my kitten (who's named Tigger and is furry and gray), my boyfriend (who's named Logan Bruno and is not furry and gray), my best friends (who are all BSC members, too), and SMS (my school, Stoneybrook Middle School). Not necessarily in that order!

What else? Oh, I'm thirteen and in eighth grade. I'm pretty shy, which makes it all the more strange that I'm the only BSC member with a steady boyfriend. My friends tease me about being "too sensitive." I have to admit, I *do* tend to cry a lot, especially at movies. I once took some kids to see *Beauty and the Beast*. You know when the Beast dies and Belle says she loves him as the last petal falls from the rose? Well, the kids were laughing hysterically during that part — because I honked when I blew my nose from crying!

I don't mind the teasing, though. My friends aren't the least bit mean. We're all so close, we can take each other seriously *and* joke about our personalities. It's funny, but my two best friends in the BSC are anything but shy. One of them also happens to be my stepsister. Her name is Dawn Schafer. We were friends even before we were family. In fact, we were the ones who got our parents together.

It's kind of a romantic story. Dawn used to live in California with her parents and younger brother, Jeff. But when her parents got divorced, her mom decided to move back to her hometown — namely, Stoneybrook.

Well, my dad grew up here, too. In fact, he

4

was in the same class as Sharon (Mrs. Schafer). In fact, he knew her. In *fact* . . . well, Dawn and I got hold of their high school yearbook, and we read these notes they'd written to each other — love letters. Yes, they had been sweethearts! At first I couldn't believe it. Sharon is sort of, well, absent-minded. (I'd use a stronger word, but I have to remember my resolution.) She's really a wonderful person, but she's been known to leave her gloves in the freezer, her keys in the bathroom soap-dish, stuff like that. My dad, on the other hand, bought a new pair of white socks last week and marked the toes with Xs so they wouldn't get mixed up in the laundry with his older white socks. He is Mr. Neatness.

With a little nudging from Dawn and me, Dad and Sharon started dating again, and the old romance must have come back. (It took a while, though, and I can imagine why. My dad has these *habits*, like bringing a calculator to restaurants to check if the waiter added correctly on the bill.) Eventually they got married, and the Schafers and Spiers became one family.

By that time, Jeff had moved back to California. (He never did adjust to Stoneybrook, and he missed his dad terribly.) So Sharon and Dawn had been living all alone in this big old farmhouse. And I mean *old*. Can you believe it was built in the 1790s? It even has a secret passageway that was once used by slaves escaping north on the Underground Railroad. The passageway leads from the barn right to Dawn's bedroom. Since my dad and I lived in a much smaller house, we moved into the farmhouse.

I love having a big family. I know four people in one house isn't exactly huge, but it's twice the size of my family beforehand. I'm an only child, and my mom died when I was little. So it was just me and Dad till I was twelve. Now, he's a caring father, but boy, was he strict. I used to have to wear my hair in pigtails and dress in conservative clothes, and I couldn't have pierced ears. I understand now that he was just being overprotective. He felt pressure to be a mother *and* a father. Sure enough, when he married Sharon, he loosened up a lot. (But I still can't have pierced ears. Sigh.)

I used to think I'd be in college before Dad let me even look at a boy. But guess what? Dad doesn't mind Logan. In fact, he likes him! Well, Logan is impossible not to like. First of all, he's super cute. His hair is dark blond and curly, his eyes are a deep blue, and he has an athletic build without looking like a jock. He's outgoing and friendly, but also thoughtful and sensitive (which he would never admit).

It hasn't been that easy for Logan and me, though. When we first started going out, Logan tended to make all the decisions and treat me as if I didn't have an independent mind. We split up for awhile, but when I talked to him about it, he really understood. Ever since then, we've been on fairly equal footing.

Logan was definitely on my mind as I stared out the Arnolds' kitchen window. Frost had made an oval frame on each windowpane, and icicles hung down like fangs. No, it wasn't the fangs that made me think of Logan. I was just daydreaming . . . imagining a sleigh ride with him, or building a snowman, *something* that would make this day seem less dreary. Stoneybrook is a nice, shady, pretty place normally, but in this weather it's like the Siberian tundra. (Not that I've ever actually been to the Siberian tundra, but it's supposed to be frigid there. The name even sounds cold.)

With a sigh, I turned away from the basement door and back to this impossible problem in my textbook. Then . . .

CRASSHHH! came a noise from the basement.

Clonk! came a note from the piano.

Knock! Knock! Knock! came the sound of Marilyn's heels against the living-room floor as she stomped to the kitchen and yelled, "Stop it, Carolyn!"

I ran to the top of the basement stairs and called down, "Are you okay?"

"Don't come down yet!" was Carolyn's answer. I guess that meant she was all right.

"Will you guys *please* stop shouting?" Marilyn shouted. She returned to the living room.

"Sorry!" Carolyn shouted back.

More powder-face music began, and more tinkering noises came from downstairs.

I once read an article about identical twins who were separated at birth. They didn't meet until they were grown-ups — but they turned out to have the same personalities, to like the same things, weigh the same, and so on. Well, Carolyn and Marilyn have been together every day of their lives, and they couldn't be more different. And it's not only that one likes music and the other science. Marilyn is kind of bossy, she dresses simply and wears her hair long, and her bedroom is decorated in yellow. Carolyn wears trendy clothes and has short hair. *Her* bedroom is almost all blue, with a kind of "cat" motif.

Up till a year ago, their parents used to dress them completely alike. The girls slept in the same bedroom and shared the same toys and books. And boy, did they have problems getting along! They even ran masking tape down the center of the room to divide it in two, so each could have her own half. I ended up having a long talk with Mrs. Arnold, and she agreed to let them have separate rooms — and separate personalities. Now they're friends, more or less.

All of a sudden the music stopped, and I heard Marilyn's footsteps rushing toward the kitchen. "I'm done," she said.

"Great," I replied. "Want to do something fun?"

Marilyn nodded. "Yeah, let's go downstairs."

"Well, Carolyn's working on this project — "

"The time machine," Marilyn said casually. "I know all about it." She ran to the top of the basement stairs, and called down, "Hey! Are you done yet?"

"No way!" Carolyn replied.

"Well, can me and Mary Anne come down?"

There was a pause. "What's the password, Marilyn?"

Marilyn exhaled. "I forgot."

"Warp movement!" Carolyn whispered loudly.

"Oh, yeah, warp movement," Marilyn repeated.

"Okay, come on," Carolyn replied.

I held back a laugh. Carolyn may have been a good scientist, but she was a terrible secret-keeper. We walked down the wooden steps to a large, unfinished basement. It had cinderblock walls and a concrete floor, with exposed pipes hanging from a low ceiling. I had to duck to avoid cobwebs.

There was a boiler against the far wall. To one of its pipes, Carolyn had tied ropes and wires. They fanned out in a kind of network, attached on the other side to a stack of wooden crates. Scraps of metal, tinfoil, crumpled-up paper, and tools were strewn around the floor. Nailed to the crates was a cardboard sign that looked like this:

"What a mess," Marilyn mumbled.

"Hello?" I said.

Carolyn popped out from behind the crates. She was wearing a pair of cat's-eye sunglasses, and the "flux capacitator" was strapped to her forehead with a terrycloth headband.

"When I am finished, you will go where no girl has gone before," Carolyn said, in a voice like a TV announcer, "to enter the final dimension, through a warp of time — "

Marilyn was practically shrieking with laughter. "Carolyn, *you're* warped!" she said.

At that moment, the boiler clicked and made a whooshing sound. Carolyn screamed and jumped away, knocking over some more crates that were off to the side. Marilyn laughed even louder.

Carolyn had landed on the floor, her glasses hanging from one ear, the headband over her eyes. I put my hand over my mouth, but it was too late. A little snort came out.

That was enough. Carolyn cracked a smile, then let out a giggle. And then, in the next instant, the three of us were rolling on the floor with laughter.

CHAPTER 2

I left the Arnolds' house at 5:19. That gave me eleven minutes. Precisely. It's a pretty long walk to Bradford Court, so I mapped out the quickest route in my head. I had worn my Keds, because I knew I'd have to move fast. Slinging my backpack securely over my shoulders, I set off.

Sound like I was going to a meeting of some secret society? Some spy organization where latecomers were locked out? Well, not exactly. I was on my way to Claudia Kishi's house for a Baby-sitters Club meeting, and I hate to be late.

By the time I got there, I felt like a walking block of ice. Usually when I reach the Kishis', I slow down a little. I take a look at the house across the street, where my dad and I used to live. I remember all the fun times I had with Claudia and Kristy (Kristy used to live next door). All these warm feelings rush through me. Well, that afternoon I had only one cold feeling: *Get inside.* Luckily, Claud leaves her front door open on meeting days, so I barged right in.

A warm, gingery smell floated out from the kitchen. I called out, "Ha, Muzz Kush!" (It was supposed to be "Hi, Mrs. Kishi," but my jaw was frozen.)

"Hello, Mary Anne!" came Mrs. Kishi's voice as I ran up the stairs. As usual, I could hear Claudia's older sister, Janine the Genius, clicking away at her computer in her bedroom. I dashed past the racket and into Claud's room.

"Hi," I said, stepping around candy wrappers, cut-up pieces of cardboard, and some string. (Claudia is very creative, and very messy.) I sneaked a look at the clock, which said 5:27.

Whew. Three minutes to spare. I had made it.

"Hi," everyone replied.

I took off my pack and sat on the bed between Claudia and Dawn. Jessica Ramsey, another of our members, was sitting on the floor. She was holding a box of Milk Duds and was tossing one up and trying to catch it in her mouth.

"Ow," Jessi said as a Dud bonked her under the nose.

"No, no," said Kristy Thomas. "Watch."

Kristy was in her usual position, sitting on a director's chair, next to the clock. She took a Milk Dud from a box in her hand, threw it almost up to the ceiling, and caught it cleanly in her mouth. "Think of your mouth as a catcher's mitt," she said.

Ew. Can you imagine?

So, we had a couple of minutes in which to relax (and thaw out) before starting time. Claudia and Dawn were looking at fashion magazines, and Kristy was coaching Jessi in Dud-catching, so I decided to pick up our record book from the floor and prepare myself in case a client called right away. (As BSC secretary, I'm in charge of the records.)

The club is a real business. Meetings begin at five-thirty sharp every Monday, Wednesday, and Friday, and they last till six. We take phone calls from parents who need sitters. Then we schedule the jobs among ourselves (there are seven regular members, and two associates). We also talk and eat and laugh and hang out. (That's why we call the BSC a "club" and not a "company" or something.)

Each of us is an officer with special duties. In the record book, I keep a calendar of all our jobs, a list of clients' addresses and phone numbers, a record of how much we've been paid, and special information about our

14

charges (problems, interests, favorite activities). It's a lot of work, but I like making lists and organizing things (I guess I get that from my dad).

By the way, there's also a BSC *notebook*, where we write descriptions of our jobs — funny stories, words of advice, anything that might help in the future.

When the BSC first started, we put fliers in supermarkets and other public places. But, as Kristy says, "Word of mouth is the best advertising," and she's right. By now, lots of Stoneybrook parents know about us. We're reliable and *very* convenient. Imagine if you were a parent. Would you rather call a bunch of sitters, one by one, hoping to find someone available — or make one call and reach seven eager, experienced sitters at once?

Do we do anything besides baby-sit? Yes, lots. We hold special events for our charges, like parties, fund drives for good causes, and picnics.

I have to admit, most of our best ideas have come from Kristy Thomas. She's like a faucet — new ideas just flow out of her all the time. Some of them are elaborate, like the time she organized a softball team made up of kids not ready for Little League. Other ideas are simple, like Kid-Kits. Those are activity boxes we take with us on sitting jobs. They're just cartons full of old toys and games and books, but believe it or not, kids *adore* them.

Kristy's *greatest* idea was . . . the Baby-sitters Club! She got the idea back in seventh grade when she and I were next-door neighbors. Her mom was frantically trying to line up a sitter for Kristy's little brother and was making a million phone calls. Suddenly the Idea Faucet started flowing. *Kristy* got on the phone — to me and Claudia. She told us her plan, and next thing you know, history was made!

Kristy, by the way, is the BSC president. (Surprised?) That means she runs the meetings and gets to scowl at whoever comes late. She's very confident and take-charge. A lot of people find her loud and bossy (well, she *is*), but the great thing about Kristy is she knows it and doesn't care. Sigh. I always wanted to be that way, but I just crumble if someone even gives me a cross look.

Remember when I said that Dawn was one of my two best friends? Kristy is the other. We've known each other since before we could walk. Now I can walk fine, but Kristy's gone on to other things — like track, softball, gymnastics, and volleyball. Unlike me, she's a great athlete. You can tell just by looking at her. She's sort of small and wiry, and always dressed in a sweat shirt and jeans.

Most people think we look alike. I'm almost as short as Kristy is, and we both have brown eyes and longish brown hair. The difference is, you would *never* mistake me for an athlete. And although I wear pretty casual clothes, I dress up a teeny bit more than she does. (For instance, that day I was wearing teal-colored stirrup pants and a bulky ski sweater with a colorful snowflake print, over a pink turtleneck.)

Kristy moved away from Bradford Court for the same reason I did — to join a stepfamily. Her natural father walked out on her family when she was six. He just left without an explanation, not long after Kristy's brother David Michael was born. For years, Mrs. Thomas somehow raised four kids (Kristy has two older brothers, Charlie and Sam) and held a full-time job. Then she fell in love with this nice, quiet guy named Watson Brewer, who happened to be very wealthy. Before we knew it, they had married and Kristy was moving into a mansion! Since then, the Thomas/Brewer family has grown. Now it includes an adopted Vietnamese girl named Emily Michelle (she's two and a half); Kristy's grandmother, who moved in to help take care of Emily; and a dog, a cat, and two goldfish.

"Hi, guys!" said Stacey McGill, as she raced into the room with Mallory Pike.

Before anyone could answer, Kristy boomed

out, "This meeting will come to order!"

Claud's digital clock had just clicked to five-thirty. Stacey and Mal quickly found places to sit, then peeled off their down coats.

"Any new business?" Kristy asked.

I told the story about Carolyn's time machine, which made everybody laugh. Stacey talked a little about the January Jamboree, an SMS dance that was coming up.

Then, when we hit a lull, Claudia got off the bed and reached behind her night table. "Hey, dudes, who wants Duds?" she said, pulling out some boxes of Milk Duds.

I should explain that Claud is a Junk Food Squirrel. She's always hiding candy bars, cookies, chips, and pretzels. Sometimes she even forgets where they are. She'll be feeling around in the back of her closet for a paintbrush or a Nancy Drew book, and — *crrunch!* — there are last April's tortilla chips! Nancy Drews, by the way, are the other things she has to hide. She's addicted to them, but her parents disapprove. They think Claud should only read classics. It's been hard for them to realize Claudia doesn't have an I.Q. of 196 like Janine. But lately they've been coming around. Claudia is an amazing artist. She paints, sculpts, draws, and makes jewelry. And her parents have finally started realizing how special that is.

Claud is the BSC vice-president. She doesn't have many official duties, but since we use her room and her private phone line, she ends up answering calls from parents who telephone at odd times. She's also *very* generous with her junk food.

You know how some people can eat anything and still stay thin? That's Claudia. Her figure is like a model's. She also has silky jet-black hair and perfect skin and dark almond-shaped eyes. (Did I mention she's Japanese-American?) As if that weren't enough, she has a fantastic sense of fashion. She can put together the oddest collection of clothes — a slouch hat, a sequined vest, an oversized button-down shirt, stirrup pants, and lace-up boots — and she looks *stunning*. If I dressed like that, people would laugh. I want to know how Claudia does it. Is she just beautiful, or can a person *learn* to look sensational?

"Let's see, I know there are some oat-bran pretzels around here somewhere . . ." Claudia was saying. Half her body was under the bed now. Her magazines were in a stack next to me and the top one was open to a page that said, "Cool and sassy for spring!" I saw pictures of models with short haircuts and gorgeous, loose-fitting clothes. I decided to take a look.

"Wow," I said, leafing through one of the

magazines. Some of the outfits were really cool. One was this long, flowing, pastel paisley print shift with a scoop neck, cinched at the waist. "This is *beautiful* . . ." I said with a sigh.

Around me, jaws were working hard on Milk Duds. "Mmph," was Kristy's reaction.

"She looks so unhappy," Jessi commented, glancing at one of the models.

Dawn giggled. "I'd love to see you in that, Mary Anne. Your face would match the color of the dress."

"You couldn't wear sneakers with it," Kristy said with a mischievous grin, after swallowing her Milk Duds.

Oh, well, so much for that idea.

"Here they are!" Claudia shouted, pulling out two bags of sesame-seed-covered, low-sodium, oat-bran pretzels. "One for Dawn, one for Stacey."

Yes, it's true. My stepsister, Dawn Schafer, likes health food. Tofu, alfalfa sprouts, carrot-parsley cocktails, millet croquettes. She actually looks forward to these things. She won't touch red meat and hardly ever eats dessert. It's weird, I know, but I love her anyway.

What does Dawn look like? Like a "California girl"! Wait, Dawn hates when people say that. I should say she looks like the *stereotype* of a California girl. She has *long* blonde hair, blue eyes, clear skin, and a trim figure.

Dawn is a real individualist. (You'd have to be, to eat teriyaki tofu loaf on a whole-wheat bun while everyone around you was eating cheeseburgers!) She does what she wants to do without worrying what others think.

Dawn doesn't have many official duties during our meetings. She's our alternate officer, which means she has to take over the job of anybody who's absent. I think she's done each job at least once.

For a long time, Dawn took over Stacey McGill's job as treasurer. That was when Stacey temporarily moved back to her hometown, New York City. Then Stacey returned to Stoneybrook, and we were all thrilled (especially Dawn, who hated being treasurer). Stacey's a real math whiz. Her job is to collect dues on Mondays, put the money in our treasury, and pay our expenses. That means helping Claudia with her phone bill, paying Kristy's brother Charlie for driving her to meetings (the Brewers live on the other side of town), and buying occasional new supplies for Kid-Kits. We grumble about paying dues. But sometimes there's enough money in the treasury for us to have a pizza party or a sleepover, and then the grumbling stops — for a little while.

I didn't tell you the reason Stacey finally moved back to Stoneybrook. You see, their return to New York was supposed to be permanent, but Stacey's parents ended up getting a divorce, and they let Stacey decide where she would live — in New York with her father or in Stoneybrook with her mother. And Stacey decided to move back to Stoneybrook. (I'm glad she did, but you know what? I'd have picked New York. I think it's the most exciting place in the world!)

Stacey is the BSC's other blonde (but a darker tint). Like Claudia, she's a fashion plate, except her style isn't as . . . *exuberant*. It's more urban and sophisticated. Like Dawn, she doesn't touch junk food. But she has a different reason. Stacey is a diabetic, which means her body can't regulate sugar in her bloodstream. If she has too much sugar (or too little), she could faint or go into a coma. So she has to take it easy with sweets and give herself daily injections of something called insulin. (Just *thinking* about that makes me shiver. If I ever saw her do it, I'd pass out!)

The phone rang, and Claudia grabbed it. "Hello, Baby-sitters Club . . . oh, hi, Mrs. Wilder! Uh-huh . . . okay, I'll check and call you right back." She hung up and turned to me. "Rosie Wilder next Tuesday, right after school?"

I put down the magazine and opened the record book. "Um . . . Jessi and Kristy are free."

"I don't know . . ." Kristy said. (Rosie is sort of a genius, and a little hard to tolerate sometimes.)

"I'll take it," Jessi chimed in. "Last time we did *barre* exercises together. It was fun."

Jessica Ramsey is one of our two junior officers, along with Mallory Pike. Why junior? Well, they're both in sixth grade, while the rest of us are in eighth. They do everything we do, except take late sitting jobs (their parents have strict curfews).

Jessi and Mal are best friends, and they have a lot in common. Both of them are the oldest in their families, both like to read, and both are convinced their parents treat them like babies. Oh, and both are *great* baby-sitters.

Other than that, they're pretty different. Jessi's black, and she has these long, graceful dancer's legs. Her hair is always pulled back from her face. Mal is white, with curly red hair, and she wears glasses (which she hates, but her parents won't let her have contacts) and braces (clear, so you don't notice them much).

Jessi has an eight-year-old sister named Becca and a baby brother named Squirt, while

Mal has *seven* siblings, including triplets!

Their interests are different, too. Jessi is a ballerina. She's so natural on stage, and her technique is incredible. She's danced lead roles in some important ballets in Stamford, the nearest big city.

Mal's talent, on the other hand, is thinking up stories. She wants to write and illustrate children's books someday.

Let's see, that brings me to our associate officers — Shannon Kilbourne and . . . saving the best for last . . . Logan Bruno! Usually they take jobs we can't fill, either because we're too booked or someone is sick.

Yes, in addition to all his other qualities, Logan is a fantastic baby-sitter. He's kind and funny and very patient.

Okay, I admit, I'm biased.

But it's true.

I flipped through to the end of Claudia's magazine. I was just about ready to shut it, when this picture caught my eye.

You know how you see models with these gorgeous haircuts, and you know you'd look *terrible* in them, but then all of a sudden, one just hits you? A cut you'd never have dreamed of getting, but when you see it on the page, you know it's just right for you?

It was in the back of *Seventeen*. It was pretty short, sort of a bowl cut in front, but really close-cropped at the neck. Very twenties (well, that's what the caption said).

Here's what I thought: All my life, I've had this long, mousy brown hair that just sort of *hangs*. The idea of feeling air on my neck was really exciting. Here's what else I thought: My New Year's resolution was to be "the best person in all possible ways" — and didn't that mean looking my best? Sure it did.

"I wonder how I'd look with this cut," I said. I was talking to myself, but Claudia was looking over my shoulder.

"Aaaaaugh!" Claudia screamed, putting her hands on her cheeks like that kid in *Home Alone*. "Not *our* Mary Anne!"

Dawn laughed and shook her head. "Please . . ."

Stacey took a peek, looked at me, and giggled.

"What?" I said. "What's so funny?"

"Well, it's . . . it's not *you*, Mary Anne," Stacey said. I know she didn't mean it, but she sounded as if she were trying to explain something to a child.

Even Jessi and Mal had these impish smiles on their faces.

With a shrug, I closed the magazine. "Well, I guess not . . ."

Maybe I was even less fashion-conscious than I had thought. But my friends' reactions made me feel strange. I felt as if they were laughing at me. What was wrong with wanting to try something new? Lots of people do it.

I told myself it wasn't a big deal, but for the rest of the meeting I said maybe two words.

CHAPTER 3

By the end of dinner that night, I was up to maybe fifty words. Both Dawn and my dad had asked if I was okay. Both times I had said yes. (The other forty-eight words had included, "Please pass the salad," and things like that.)

At first I couldn't figure out why I felt so grumpy. I thought maybe it was the cold weather. Then I thought it was something I had eaten. But the real reason didn't come to me until I was in my bedroom later, alone.

As I was brushing Tigger's fur, all I could think about was the BSC meeting. That dumb little incident was still on my mind.

I kept picturing that model with the hairstyle I liked. Stacey had said, "It's not you, Mary Anne."

That's all. Not a terrible insult, right? People say that kind of thing all the time.

Still, it was sticking in my mind like a piece of bubble gum under a tabletop. How could Stacey know what was "me"? How could Claudia, or even Dawn?

I picked up a little hand mirror. Looking into it, I tried to see "me."

I saw a decent, neat-looking girl with sort of blah hair and a gloomy face. I forced a smile, but that made "me" look worse.

Okay, so "me" wasn't so hot. No big deal. Not everyone can be a super-model.

Still, I wondered what everyone had found so funny. I reached behind my neck and pulled my hair up. I tried to imagine what that short haircut would look like.

Have you ever taken a really good look at your jaw? I never had, until I was staring at myself with my hair up. My attention went right to it. And you know what? I kind of liked it. It had a strong curve. It wasn't too thin or too broad. I mean, all my life I'd always noticed the normal things in the mirror — my eyes, teeth, hair, lips, skin. They're all okay, but not beautiful. Now I was discovering a new part of me. Mary Anne's Beauty Secret.

The Jaw that Launched a Thousand Ships.

I giggled at that thought. My mirror image giggled back. I couldn't believe what I was seeing.

I looked *great* with short hair!

Maybe this really was "me." Maybe all these years I just never allowed the real Mary Anne to come out.

Then it dawned on me. It didn't matter that my friends laughed. *I* laughed when I saw my hair up. A drastic change is always a little shock, and shocks make you laugh.

I tried to imagine what my friends would do if I came to a meeting with short hair. Sure, they'd probably giggle and make comments at first. But what fun it would be when they realized how nice I looked! The idea gave me a shiver of excitement.

I opened the bottom drawer of my desk, which is my own special hiding place (I got the idea from Claudia). I took out a few fashion magazines I'd stashed there. They were a couple of months old, but I leafed through them anyway.

In the second one, I found the haircut. Well, not the exact one, but close enough. In fact, this model was a little more my type. She had brown hair and a friendly face, and she wasn't bone-thin like the model in Claudia's magazine.

That was when I made my decision. I *was* going to get my hair cut. I owed it to myself. I owed it to my New Year's resolution. I would find a good hair salon, show them the picture, and go through with it.

But there was one big "if." *If* I could convince my dad.

My stomach sank. Convincing him to let me take my hair out of pigtails had been almost impossible. Sure, he wasn't as strict now as he used to be, but still . . .

I carefully ripped the page out of the magazine. Maybe if I showed him exactly what I wanted to do, he'd be more likely to give me permission.

But before I went downstairs, I'd have to do some homework. I didn't want him to say, "Now, young lady, you shouldn't be looking at magazines during your work time."

At precisely nine o'clock, after some social studies and math, I shut my notebook, grabbed the magazine photo, and ran downstairs.

Dad was alone in the living room, reading the newspaper. I could hear Sharon on the phone in the kitchen.

"Hi," I said nonchalantly.

Dad looked up and smiled. "Hi! You look happier than before."

"Oh! Yeah, I think the weather was getting me down," I said. Then I took the plunge. "Um, Dad . . . can I show you something?"

"Sure."

I held out the picture. "What do you think of this haircut?"

Dad looked at it, scratching his chin. "Um . . . very spiffy." (He's always using words like that.) "Why?"

"Well, I was thinking . . . it looks kind of pretty . . . and I need a trim anyway . . ."

"You mean, you want to get a cut like *this* for yourself?" Dad said, taking the magazine to look closer.

I nodded meekly. "Yeah. Don't you think it'd be a nice change?"

Dad drummed his fingers against his chin. I had an awful feeling. A scary image popped into my head. He'd get so angry, he'd never let me cut my hair again. I'd be like Rapunzel. I pictured my hair growing down to my feet, with split ends that started at my waist.

But Dad exhaled and nodded. "I think you would look lovely."

Huh?

I didn't think I was hearing right. My dad does have a kind of strange, quiet sense of humor. Sometimes I can't tell if he's joking. "You . . . you mean it?"

Dad chuckled. "Yes, I mean it. I always thought short hair would suit you. I was under the impression *you* didn't like it."

"Oh, Dad!" I cried, throwing my arms around him.

"Now, if you want it really short," he said with a sly smile, "there's a fellow at Frank's Barber Shop . . ."

"*Daaad*," I replied. "I was thinking of that salon at Washington Mall, where Stacey got her perm."

"Isn't that kind of far? What about the place in town?"

"No!" I said. "They destroyed poor Karen Brewer's hair." (It's true, too. The place is called Gloriana's House of Hair, but it might as well be called Gloriana's House of Horror.)

"Well, we wouldn't want that," Dad said. "What are you doing Saturday?"

"Um . . . you know, nothing special."

"How about a father-daughter day? We haven't done that in a long time. I'll take you to the salon, then we can browse around the mall, have some lunch, just . . . hang out."

I can't help laughing when my dad uses expressions like *hang out*. He kind of wiggles his head awkwardly, like he's trying to be hip. But no matter. I was *thrilled*. "That would be so much fun!"

"Let me just make sure Sharon doesn't need me to — "

"Oh, Dad? One other thing. I want to keep the haircut a secret. Even from Dawn and Sharon."

"Why?"

"To surprise them. I can't wait to see the expressions on their faces!"

Dad gave me a wink. "All right, my lips are sealed."

"Thanks," I said, giving him a kiss on the cheek.

I ran upstairs. Suddenly I felt great. I finished my homework in no time. I talked to Dawn a little about Carolyn's time machine, I talked to Logan on the phone about going to the January Jamboree together. And I never *once* mentioned my haircut.

The Official Countdown had begun. It was T minus three days until the New Mary Anne!

CHAPTER 4

Monday

Saturday I sat
for the Arnold
twins. Mary Anne
had told me about
Carolyn's contraption.
I really wanted
to see it. I even
asked my mom to
rent Back to the Future
Friday night, just
to get into the
spirit.

Well, I kind
of imagined Carolyn
would be like
Michael J. Fox.
But to tell you
the truth, she
was more like
the guy who
played the mad
scientist ...

Jessi was the perfect person to sit for the twins. Because of her ballet, she knows some classical music, which helps Marilyn. And Jessi's also read a lot of science fiction, so she could talk about time travel with Carolyn.

They were in the kitchen, having lunch, when Jessi mentioned *Back to the Future*. Well, forget it. Carolyn was off and running.

"Did you like the part where his mom calls him Calvin Klein, 'cause she sees that name on his underwear?" Carolyn said, laughing so hard a piece of lettuce shot out of her mouth.

"Say it, don't spray it," Marilyn mumbled.

"That was pretty funny," Jessi said, answering Carolyn. "How about the part where Dr. Brown laughs hysterically when Marty tells him Ronald Reagan will be President one day."

"It's my *favy-avy-avorite* movie of all time!" Carolyn said.

Marilyn yawned. "We know that."

"Well, you said you liked it, too," Carolyn insisted. Then she barged ahead, turning to Jessi. "I know a lot about time travel. You know what I started to read? *The Time Machine*."

"Dad has to read most of it to her," Marilyn cut in.

"It's soooo exciting," Carolyn said.

"I read that," Jessi said. "It's by H. G. Wells."

"Yeah, that's him!"

"I've been reading this great book called *Time and Again*, by a guy named Jack Finney," Jessi said. "It's about a secret government project, where people go back in time to change history."

Carolyn's eyes widened. "Wow! Is there really such a thing?"

Jessi laughed. "I don't think so . . ."

"There could be!" Carolyn insisted. "I saw a TV show that said there are, um, like warps in space that have these wormholes — "

Marilyn squealed with laughter. *"Worm-holes?"*

"Yeah!" Carolyn said with a pout.

"So that means *worms* can travel in space?"

"Not in space. In *time*, dodo brain!"

"You can't call me that!"

"And not just worms — anything can! Except maybe you, 'cause you're too — "

Jessi the Peacemaker took over. "If you really could go back in time, what time would you go to?"

The girls fell silent for a moment. "Back to when my mom and dad were kids," Carolyn said. "I could baby-sit for them."

"And make them eat broccoli!" Marilyn added.

The girls giggled. Jessi could tell Marilyn was finally interested in the conversation. "How about you, Marilyn?" Jessi asked.

Marilyn thought deeply. "Oh, the late 1700s."

"Why?"

"Then I could, like, hide Mozart's pencils or something, so he wouldn't write such hard music."

That wasn't what Jessi had expected. She laughed.

"How about you, Jessi?" Carolyn said.

"I'd go to Paris in the early 1900s," Jessi volunteered, "to see this great ballet dancer named Nijinsky. They say he was so exciting to watch that people would faint in the audience."

"Wow," Marilyn said.

Carolyn had a mischievous glint in her eye. "Well, maybe you *can* see him!" She jumped up from her chair. "Follow me!"

Carolyn led Jessi and Marilyn down to the basement. (No password was required.) There, in all its high-tech glory, was the time machine. According to Jessi, it looked exactly the way it had looked when I saw it — the crates, the ropes tied to the boiler, the sign with the bad spelling.

"Bet you don't know what this is," Carolyn said.

"It's a time machine," Marilyn piped up.

"*Marilyn . . .*"

"That's exactly what I thought it was!" Jessi said. "It looks . . . great."

"I still need a few parts," Carolyn said. She rummaged around on the floor and found a neatly folded piece of paper. "Here's my list."

She held out the paper for Jessi to see. It looked like this:

Top Secret
Chek List for Time Mashin
Dr. Carolyn Arnold, Scientist

Flux Capasitatter
Warp Consol
The Hands from A Brokened Clock
Unpluged Telephone
Old Blankit
Dish Towl
Some Toylet Paper
One Curtain Rod

"Some of these might be a little hard to find," Carolyn said.

Jessi's baby-sitting instinct took over. A search would be a perfect activity. "I bet we can find these things," she said. "Let's go on a scavenger hunt!"

"Yeah!" Carolyn and Marilyn cried.

They ran upstairs. "The dish towels are in the pantry!" Marilyn said, running into the kitchen.

"I'll get the toilet paper!" Carolyn called out.

Jessi stood in the kitchen, looking at the list. "Where do you keep old blankets?"

Marilyn rushed over, holding a faded old dish towel. "Top shelf of the linen closet," she said. "I'll show you."

She and Jessi ran to a narrow closet in the hallway between the kitchen and the living room. Sure enough, a motheaten woolen blanket sat on the top shelf. Jessi took it down and went back to the kitchen, to put it on the table.

Carolyn was already bunching up a big wad of toilet paper.

"Where do you keep all the stuff you don't want?" Jessi asked.

"The attic," Carolyn answered. "But it's scary up there."

"I'm not scared!" Marilyn said. "Let's go."

Carolyn couldn't stay downstairs after that. The three of them barged into the attic.

It *was* a little creepy, but right in the middle of it was a huge box filled with old baby toys. And on the top was a toy telephone on wheels.

"There's our unplugged telephone!" Jessi said.

"Look," Carolyn exclaimed, pulling out a

radio alarm clock with fake wood paneling. "Remember this? Mom called it a piece of junk and Dad said to save it."

The cover of the clock face was missing, and the hands were dangling. Carolyn pulled them off. "They won't even notice," she said.

"Our old shower curtain!" Marilyn exclaimed from under one of the attic eaves. She held up a metal rod with crinkly plastic curtains.

Jessi checked the list. "Great, that's the last thing! Let's go!"

"Back to the basement!" Carolyn said.

They clattered down two flights of stairs, grabbing all their supplies. When they reached the machine, Carolyn lined up everything carefully on the floor. Then she went to work.

"Let's see," she said, wrapping the toilet paper around her magnifying glass. "The flux capacitator must have a cushion from warp shock . . . the curtain rod will conduct the electricity . . . now, if we set the hands to a specific time . . ."

It didn't take Marilyn long to grow bored. "I'm going to go read," she said, trudging back upstairs.

Jessi stayed in the basement. Carolyn tinkered around, attaching things to the crates, adjusting the wires. All the time she kept mumbling to herself, as if Jessi weren't even there.

A weird thought crossed Jessi's mind: What if Carolyn really believed this stuff?

But she just smiled and threw that thought away. Carolyn was old enough to know fantasy from reality.

"Perfect!" Carolyn said. She turned to Jessi, her face aglow. "We'll be ready for our first trip by next week!"

Then again, maybe not.

CHAPTER 5

Santa rose slowly upward, then disappeared. He was still checking his list. Beside him, a girl with tennis shorts happily sniffed a bunch of daisies. She didn't take any notice of him.

It was the Changing of the Window Displays at Washington Mall. (Santa and the girl were mannequins.)

While Jessi was sitting for the Arnold twins, Dad and I were looking at the window of Steven E, one of the mall's fanciest clothing boutiques. After yanking Santa out of the way, the designers began setting up a spring garden scene around the girl. One of them saw us and started dancing with another mannequin.

Dad and I laughed. "The clothes here are *sooo* nice," I said. "But really expensive."

"Well, let's get your hair cut first," Dad said. "Let's see how much that costs. Then maybe we can go in."

I didn't expect him to say that. In fact, I felt a little guilty. Maybe Dad thought I had been hinting for him to take me into that store.

I hadn't been, but I have to admit I was thrilled he had offered.

We rode the mall elevator to the floor where the salon was. When we went in, I asked for Joyce (Stacey's favorite hairstylist). I was in luck. She was there, just finishing up a customer.

Unfortunately, that customer was a very old lady with bluish-white hair, all done up in a kind of beehive. I was having second thoughts about Joyce.

As we sat in the waiting area, I could hear Dad making sniffing noises. "What is that smell?" he said.

"Someone's getting a perm," I replied.

"Oh," he said with a slightly sour expression.

I reached into my bag and took out the photo of the haircut I wanted. Dad rummaged through a pile of fashion magazines, before he found a three-month-old issue of *Rolling Stone*. "I don't suppose I'd find *The Wall Street Journal* here," he muttered.

In a few minutes, a young woman motioned me over to the sinks in the corner of the salon. The warmth of the water calmed me down. As I was being towel-dried, I noticed Joyce's customer was standing up and admiring her beehive. Joyce smiled at me and said, "Your turn."

This was It. There was no turning back now.

I stood up and caught a glimpse of myself in the mirror. My hair cascaded to my shoulders. Suddenly it seemed so beautiful. I thought of all the events of my life, all the ups and downs I had gone through *with this hair*. It was like an old friend. In a few minutes, most of it was going to be lying in wet clumps on the floor.

Part of me wanted to run away, but I didn't give in. This was the New Mary Anne. Willing to try new things, to be the best possible person she could be.

"Hi," I said bravely.

"What can I do for you?" Joyce asked.

I explained that I was a friend of Stacey's. Then I showed her the photo. "Can you do this style?"

Joyce looked at it, then stared at me through squinty eyes. Finally she nodded confidently. "Sure. This will look fabulous on you."

"Uh-huh," I said, settling into the chair. I tried to smile. I swallowed. I closed my eyes.

"Now, honey, this isn't the dentist's office," Joyce said.

My eyes opened and I actually smiled.

"Are you sure you want to do this?" Joyce asked.

"Yes!" I said quickly.

Joyce went to work. She tried to make conversation while she snipped away. I kept saying "Uh-huh" and laughing weakly at her jokes. I must have sounded like a real dope, but I couldn't keep my eyes off the mirror. Each hunk of falling hair was like a little death.

(I can't help it — that's how it felt!)

But you know what? When Joyce clipped off the last long strands, I changed. I saw what the hairstyle was going to look like. I said hello to my jaw again (not aloud).

When Joyce finished, I almost jumped out of my seat. I looked . . . well, let's put it this way. I did *not* look like the model, but I did look like a new person. I *felt* like one, too. I could see my grin growing and growing in the mirror. I didn't know what to say, so I sort of squealed.

"She's excited," Joyce said to my dad.

"Yes," Dad replied. He wasn't exactly bursting with praise, but he was smiling.

I could barely feel my feet touch the ground, I was so happy. I must have stared in that mirror for ages. I wanted to see every possible angle. Eventually Dad paid the cashier and gently led me away.

"Thanks!" I said to Joyce.

"My pleasure," Joyce replied. "Say hi to Stacey for me."

What a feeling came over me as I walked out of the salon. Who ever knew there were *breezes* in a mall? Well, there were, and I felt every one of them on my neck.

"Oh, thank you, Dad!" I exclaimed. "Do you like it?"

"The important thing is, do *you* like it?" he replied.

My stomach went into knots. He hadn't said *yes*. "I love it . . . but . . ." I felt my lower lip start to tremble. "You *don't* like it, do you?"

Dad gave me a concerned look. "No, I think it's wonderful, sweetheart. It makes you look like a beautiful young woman. It's just . . ." He shrugged and tried to smile. "Well, you're growing up, Mary Anne. That's never easy for a parent to see, especially an old grump like me."

So that's what it was. The look in Dad's eyes was sad and proud and happy, all at the same time. Oh boy. Now I felt like crying for a different reason.

Fortunately, a chirpy voice interrupted our silence. "Free makeover for our grand opening?"

I turned to see a stunning woman in a clingy dress. She smelled of perfume and was wearing lots of makeup. She was easily six feet tall. The store behind her had been under construction the last time I was here. Now its display window was stuffed with perfumes and cosmetics. The words *About Face* arched across the window in purple neon lights.

"It's free!" she said again. "This week only. No purchase necessary. You'll be glad you tried it."

It was exactly what I needed — an elegant makeup job to go with an elegant haircut. Of course, I was wearing no makeup at all. "Dad?" I asked.

Dad shrugged. "Why not?"

And that was how I, the New Mary Anne, found myself at the makeup counter of About Face, being fussed over by two women who could have been models themselves.

One of them thought my complexion was a "winter," another was convinced it was a "late spring." They kept holding patches of color against my cheek and nodding or shaking their heads. I had no idea what they were doing.

But I felt great.

By the time I was ready to look in a mirror, they were both grinning widely.

When I turned to see myself, I nearly gasped. I looked about seventeen years old. My cheekbones seemed higher, my eyes seemed wider, and my lips were absolutely *luscious.* The makeup was exactly right with my new hair.

"Darling, you look like you stepped off the cover of *Vogue*," one of the women said.

"Thanks," I replied, watching my face turn bright red.

"It's true," said the other. She turned to Dad and said, "What do you think of your daughter?"

This time Dad didn't hesitate. "Gorgeous!" he said proudly. "Why don't you write down the . . er, recipe you used."

Recipe? I tried not to giggle. With a straight face, one of the women took a pen and a printed sheet from the countertop. "I'll circle each of the products we used. If you wish to purchase any of them, show the salesperson this sheet and you'll get a twenty percent discount."

"Thanks," I said, taking the sheet. I gave Dad a hopeful look.

With a chuckle he said, "Oh, we've gone this far. Why not go all the way?"

We bought some blush, eyeliner, and lipstick. I could tell Dad was adding the prices up in his head, but he didn't protest one bit (and, thank goodness, he didn't take out his calculator).

On our way out we heard some jazz from

the center court of the mall. "That's a Charlie Parker tune," Dad said.

One thing about Dad. He can be very conservative, but he knows jazz. We took the elevator down and joined a crowd of people watching a five-person group — drummer, bass player, pianist, saxophonist, and a singer.

During a fast tune, I could hear this strange, muffled noise. "Eh eh eh-eh-eh-eh . . . eh eh . . ." It was starting to become annoying, until I realized it was coming from the drummer. He was playing with his eyes closed and . . . *grunting* to the music.

I caught Dad's eye, and we smiled. "Should we tell him?" he whispered.

"Dad!" I put my hand to my mouth, trying not to giggle. What if he *heard* us?

"Hey, are you as hungry as I am?" Dad suddenly asked.

"Yes," I said.

"For Mexican food?"

"Yes!"

We went to the Casa Grande and ordered heaping portions of burritos, enchiladas, and other yummy fattening stuff. Then we found a table near the jazz group, so we sat, ate, told jokes, and listened for "Eh-eh."

After lunch and jazz we both felt very mellow and slowmoving. We sauntered through the mall, window-shopping and chatting. Dad actually suggested we go into Steven E, but I felt a little guilty because he'd already spent so much money.

"Well, let's just take a look," he insisted.

When we reached the store and saw some of the price tags, Dad's eyebrows arched *way* up.

A young, well-dressed guy with moussed hair and a flashy smile was walking toward us. "Hi, I'm Steven," he said. "Don't forget, this is our post-season sale. Everything is thirty to sixty percent off the marked price. Browse around, take a look, and if you need any help, just ask."

"Thanks," Dad said.

As Steven walked away, I whispered to Dad, "It's okay, the haircut and the makeup are enough." But I couldn't take my eyes off this outfit. It was a fiery red, off-the-shoulder crepe dress, with shirred sleeves, a fitted bodice, and a skirt that flared to mid-calf. It was the kind of dress the old me would never have dreamed of wearing.

But the New Mary Anne would look great in it for the January Jamboree!

Dad, as usual, was reading my mind. "What if we strike a deal," he said. "I'll charge whatever clothes and accessories you need, but you will be responsible for paying me back half, whenever you can."

"Really?"

"Really."

"Okay, it's a deal!"

I felt like a kid who'd gone to sleep in June and awakened on Christmas Day. Since half of it was my money, I didn't get *everything* I wanted. But it was "quite a haul," as my dad said: the dress; some stockings and a pair of shoes to go with it; an oversized, indigo cable-knit sweater; and a pair of floral paisley print Lycra leggings with a French terry top.

Maybe I'd have to baby-sit every day till college to pay him back, but I didn't care. As Dad and I left the mall, we were actually singing songs aloud. What a perfect day. I felt very close to my father.

On the way home we stopped at Uncle Ed's, a Chinese restaurant, and ordered some takeout food for dinner. Even though I could practically still taste my enchiladas, the smell from our takeout bags was making me hungry again.

As we pulled up the driveway, I yanked down the passenger-seat visor to look in the mirror. I saw a tiny smudge of eyeliner by my left eye, which I wiped away. Otherwise, everything was perfect.

"Ready to introduce yourself?" Dad said with a grin.

"Ready!" My heart was beating as fast as Eh-eh's drums. I couldn't wait for Sharon and Dawn to see me.

Dad parked the car in the driveway. I grabbed the Steven E bags, ran across the lawn, and rang the bell.

Dad stepped up behind me. Sharon opened the door and looked me blankly in the face. Dawn stood next to her.

I yelled out the only word that came to mind. "Surprise!"

CHAPTER 6

Dead silence.

Dead, *stunned* silence.

And then a whispered, "Mary Anne?" from Dawn.

My stomach was fluttering like crazy. Dawn and Sharon were just staring at me. I wanted to shrink into the ground. Why didn't they *say* something — *anything*? Even if they screamed and ran away in terror, at least I'd know how they felt.

The staring probably lasted for all of two seconds, but it felt like two hours. Finally Sharon began to smile. She looked me up and down and said, "Who on earth is this gorgeous movie star?"

Oh! She liked it! My flutters fluttered away. I spun around. My new hair whipped gently across my face, then bounced back into place. "What do you think?" I asked.

"You look . . . you look *sensational!*" Sharon

said, laughing. "Now, come in! It's freezing out here and you have nothing on your neck!"

As we walked inside, I glanced over my shoulder at Dad. He was smiling from ear to ear, and he gave me a wink. Tigger scampered up to me and wound himself around my ankles.

"I'm . . . speechless!" Sharon exclaimed. "Why — what made you do this?"

"I don't know," I said with a smile. "New Year, new look . . . I figured it was time to experiment. I've been thinking about this for awhile, but I wanted to keep it a secret."

"And you were in on it, Richard?" Sharon asked.

"Sure," he said. "I was the principal source of funding."

We were in the kitchen now, and Dad put the bags of Chinese food on the table. "Anybody hungry?" he asked.

"I am," Dawn said, helping Dad take out the food containers. "What did you get?"

"Moo shu vegetables, sesame bean curd, lo mein — and some shelled lobster in oyster sauce, for the carnivores," Dad said, throwing me another smile. "To celebrate."

"Ew," Dawn said under her breath, as she opened the round aluminum tin that contained the lobster. With each tin she uncovered, a new, warm, drool-making smell flooded the kitchen. My burrito instantly became a distant memory.

"Help me set the table," Sharon said, "so we can eat before it gets cold. Then I want to hear *all* about your trip."

"Okay," I answered.

I noticed that Dawn was paying a lot of attention to the food. I also noticed she hadn't said a word about my haircut and makeover.

As I started putting plates down, Dad said to Dawn, "So, what do you think of your new stepsister?"

"I can't believe you got your hair cut, Mary Anne," she said. "Where'd you go? Gloriana's?"

"No," I replied. "You know that place Stacey went to? At the mall?"

"You went *there*? That fancy salon?"

Dad chuckled. Ladling food onto our plates, he said, "That fancy salon smelled like rotten eggs and had an equally rotten selection of magazines — but the stylists sure do nice work."

We sat down, as Sharon put chopsticks next to three of the plates (and a fork next to Dad's). "I used Stacey's hairstylist," I said. "Then I got a free makeover at this great new cosmetics store, and Dad bought me some of the makeup they used."

"They did a wonderful job," Sharon said,

studying my face. "Let's see. I'm trying to figure out what they did."

I spread out a moo-shu pancake and spooned a little plum sauce on it.

"Why didn't you tell us you were going to have a makeover?" Dawn asked me.

It was a fair question. But I felt something clench in my stomach. Dawn had not yet said anything nice. She was trying to be friendly, but something wasn't right. Did she think I looked terrible? Was she mad at me? Had I done something wrong before I left the house that morning?

"Well, I didn't really decide for sure till the last minute," I began.

"You just said you had been thinking about it for awhile," Dawn cut in.

"*Thinking* about it," I said. "But you know me — "

"I thought I did." Dawn jammed some bean curd in her mouth.

"Well . . ." I had the urge to apologize, but I knew that was silly. Apologize for what? Instead I just looked down and spread some vegetables on my pancake.

Dad began talking about the things we had seen in the mall — the man dancing with the mannequin, the jazz band, and the lunchtime scene.

The highlight was Dad's imitation of the

drummer. He tapped his fork on the table, grunting, "Eh-eh . . . eh eh eh eh."

I started laughing, and Sharon looked at us with this curious smile, as if we'd just lost our minds.

"Must have been funny," Dawn said, staring down at a cube of bean curd.

Then Dad said, "By the time we went to the clothing store, I felt like taking a nap — "

"Clothing store?" Dawn said, looking up. "You went to a clothing store, too?"

"Yes," Dad said. "That's what's in all those shopping bags. Clothes. We went to some expensive place named after a young fellow who spells his last name with one letter."

Dawn's eyes popped open. "You bought the clothes at Steven E?"

"Yes," Dad said, rolling his eyes. "A dress, a sweater, shoes . . ."

"But — but it's right after Christmas!" Dawn said. "I mean, that place is so expensive, and — "

"Oh, Mary Anne's going to pay for half," Dad replied. "And I won't forget to remind her."

Dawn shot a look at her mom. I could tell Sharon wasn't thrilled about the expense, but she didn't really look angry.

I'll never forget Dawn's expression, though. I could tell she wanted to seem nonchalant, but her face was tense. She actually looked hurt.

My excitement faded. One thing about me, whenever I sense someone doesn't like me or is mad at me, I always assume I'm wrong. Most times I start to cry. Then I try to figure out what I did and what I can do to redeem myself.

Well, that was the way I felt about Dawn just then.

I could barely concentrate during the rest of the dinner.

It was my turn to clean up the kitchen that night, and Dawn's turn to clear the table. When she picked up my plate, she didn't even look at me.

I took some glasses into the kitchen and began loading the dishwasher. When I bent down, my hair fell across my eyes. I was startled. For a split second I thought a spider had fallen on me from the ceiling. I could tell I was going to have to get used to some new sensations.

But there was one sensation I never would have predicted — I felt *guilty*.

At first I didn't know why, but soon it hit me. Dawn was jealous of me. I should have seen it right away. Why was I so dumb? I shouldn't have bragged about what Dad and I had done. I shouldn't have let him buy me so many things. I should have suggested that Dawn come with us to the mall.

My thoughts were tumbling around. I didn't know whether to talk to Dawn, or wait for her to come to me, or ask Dad's advice.

I decided to do none of the above. There was only one thing that would make me feel better at that point — talking to Logan. Just hearing his voice usually puts me in a good mood.

I quickly finished up and turned the dishwasher on. Then I sat on the stool by the wall phone and called Logan's number.

"Hello?" It was Logan's little brother, Hunter.

"Hi, Hunter," I said.

"Bary Add!" Hunter squealed. He has allergies to just about everything, so he always sounds nasal. "*Logad! Logad!* It's Bary Add! Bary Add, I got a didosaur backpack today!"

"Wow, that's great — "

"Hello? Mary Anne?"

That was Logan. I wish you could hear his voice. It's really warm and cheerful, and he has this great Southern accent. (His family moved to Stoneybrook from Louisville, Kentucky.)

"Hi," I said. "How are you?"

"Almost thawed out," he said. "Dad and I were chopping up the ice on the driveway."

"Sounds like fun."

"Think so? We should have invited you over."

"Yeah, I could have cheered you on!"

"Big help." Logan laughed. "What'd you do today?"

I wanted to tell him. I almost blurted it out. But I really wanted to wait and let him *see* it. "Um, Logan? I have a surprise for you."

I heard a faint click. I figured Hunter or Kerry (Logan's sister) probably picked up the other line at his house.

"Surprise? What is it?" Logan said.

"I can't tell you," I answered.

Then I heard Dawn's voice. "Some surprise!"

"Dawn?" I said.

"Sorry," she replied. "I picked up the other extension by — "

"What do you mean, some surprise?" Logan insisted.

"Well, it's just — " Dawn began.

"*Dawn!*" I warned.

"It's not that earth-shattering, Mary Anne," Dawn said. "I mean, we all get haircuts."

"A haircut?" Logan piped up. "You got a haircut?"

I could not believe what was happening. "Dawn, I wanted to *show* him!"

"Oh," Dawn said. "Sorry. 'Bye, Logan."

The phone clicked again, and she was gone.

Sorry was about the last thing she sounded.

"What happened?" Logan pleaded. "Did you do something crazy, like cut it all off?"

"Well," I said, "not *all*."

"But it's real short, right?"

"Yeah, but — "

"Why did you do it?"

I couldn't keep my feelings to myself anymore. "Why is everyone so upset about this?" I cried. "I was so happy! I couldn't wait to show you! Now I feel like I did some awful thing." Tears welled up in my eyes.

"Oh, Mary Anne, I'm sorry. I didn't mean to sound like that," Logan said. "It's just a shock, that's all. I can't wait to see it. Can I come over first thing tomorrow?"

"Yes," I said. "I — I have to go now."

"Okay, I'll see you around nine-thirty."

"Okay. 'Bye."

" 'Bye."

I hung up, half-expecting myself to burst into tears. That would have been the old Mary Anne's usual response. But my eyes were dry. I was annoyed. Annoyed? I was actually *angry*. How could Dawn be so rotten?

I decided I'd go into my room and wait for her to apologize. And if she didn't, fine. I had no desire to say another word to her, anyway.

CHAPTER 7

I did talk to Dawn that night. I asked, "Where's the toothpaste?" (I had to. She had brought it into her room by mistake.) But that was it.

We kept our distance on Sunday, speaking to each other only when necessary. Dawn did not apologize or even mention what had happened the evening before.

The good thing was that Logan did come over that morning. And guess what? He said he *loved* my hair! Boy, did that make me feel better.

Well, the count was in my favor: three for my new look (four including Tigger) and one against. But Monday would be the big test. The whole world would finally see the New Mary Anne.

Well, at least SMS would.

On Monday morning I put on some makeup. No, I don't ever wear makeup to school, but I thought I'd try just this once. Then I brushed my hair and used a tiny bit of hairspray.

Dawn was eating her whole-grain puffed cereal and lowfat yogurt when I sat down to breakfast. I broiled some bacon and made myself some sweet, gloppy French toast.

(I wasn't really doing it to be mean. That was what I wanted to eat, and I wasn't going to bend over backward just because that stuff turns her stomach. Besides, she was almost finished eating.)

I plopped my breakfast plate down at the table. A greasy piece of bacon slipped off. I picked it up and ate it.

"Gross," Dawn said.

"Good morning," I said.

We left separately for school.

I had butterflies as I walked into SMS. I half expected the entire eighth-grade class to be in the lobby, waiting to laugh at me.

But I got over that. I was very mature. I refused to be ruffled.

"*Ucccccchhh!* What happened to *you?*"

My ruffles came back.

Just my luck. Of all the people to run into first, it *would* have to be Alan Gray.

In case you don't know, Alan is known by many as the Jerk of Eighth Grade (and that's one of the nicer names). Why? Let's just say maturity is not his strong point. Plus he's been trying to get back at the entire BSC ever since he lost a bet to Kristy and had to be her personal slave for a week.

"Hello, Alan," I said calmly.

"Well, at least they didn't scalp off your voice box!" was Alan's witty response.

"No, they didn't," I replied, heading for the hallway. "See you."

The day was off to a wonderful start.

I managed to escape to my locker without anyone else seeing me. But just as I opened it, I heard a wolf whistle behind me.

Now I was upset. Hadn't Alan said enough already? Why did he have to follow me? I turned around, not knowing whether to yell at him or cry.

It was Logan.

"Who's the new girl?" he said with a smile.

I smiled back. "Hi. You still like it?"

"Love it. I still can't believe how *different* you look!"

With a straight face, I replied, "What was wrong with the way I looked before?"

"No — I meant — well, you know — "

"You thought I was ugly, and you didn't tell me?"

Logan had this hurt-puppy look on his face.

He was taking me so seriously. "No! I didn't mean that — "

I couldn't stand it any longer. I started to giggle.

"Ohhhh, you're in trouble." Logan wrapped his arm around my neck, pretending to get me in a headlock. I ducked away, laughing. (Logan may be a semi-jock, but he's gentle as a mouse.)

Standing just to our left were Bruce Schermerhorn and Justin Forbes, two eighth-graders I know. Their jaws were practically scraping the ground. "Mary Anne *Spier*?" Bruce said.

"Hi," I replied.

"Wow . . . hey," Bruce said.

Wow . . . hey? Well, he was smiling and nodding, so I guess that was meant to be a compliment. I said, "Thanks," and linked arms with Logan.

We walked together to my homeroom, which happens to be about twenty-seven miles away from my locker. Which meant we had to pass a lot of people on the way.

Now, finally, was the Moment of Truth. The Great Unveiling.

You know what? Some people didn't even recognize me! Erica Blumberg kept giving Logan this suspicious glance, as if he'd found a new girlfriend. Shawna Riverson walked right by me.

I'll tell you when I really started feeling good. It was when Cokie Mason actually dropped her books and gasped. (Cokie used to have a major crush on Logan. She dated him, back when he and I had split up.) "Hi, Cokie," I said nonchalantly.

"Wow, you look fantastic!" she exclaimed.

Maybe she wasn't so bad after all. She did give me my second Wow of the day.

"Thanks!" I said.

Well, "thanks" was the word I used most on the way to my homeroom. I felt like a movie star. Imagine, *me*, drab old Mary Anne! No one had ever fussed over my looks before. And now *everyone* was paying attention. One of the teachers even came out of her classroom to compliment me.

To tell you the truth, it was a little embarrassing. Logan said my face was like a blinking red stoplight. But by the time we finally turned the last corner to my homeroom, I was enjoying myself.

That was when I saw Claudia, Kristy, and Stacey. They were walking toward us, chatting. My heart started racing. I couldn't *wait* to see the looks on their faces. "Hi!" I called out.

Stacey looked up. "Hi, Mary Anne. Hi, Logan." She raised an eyebrow. "It's shorter than I thought. Did Joyce do it?"

She didn't seem surprised at all. "Yeah," I said. "Um . . . did she mention it to you or something?"

"No," Kristy said. "Dawn did."

Ooooooh. It figured. I should have specifically told her not to say anything!

Not that it would have mattered. She knew I'd wanted to surprise Logan, and that hadn't stopped her.

"I can't believe you went to the hairdresser without us," Claudia said, with a scolding sort of smile.

"I'm sorry," I replied. (I couldn't help it, the words just flew out of my mouth.) "Well, what do you think?"

Claudia and Stacey gave each other a Look. Kristy smiled and shrugged. "Mary Anne, you knucklehead . . . we *said* that cut wasn't you."

Kristy was trying to sound as if she were joking, but she meant it. I knew that tone of voice.

Some best friend.

"It's okay," Claudia said.

"It'll grow out," Stacey added.

Funny, their comments were sort of mean, but they didn't *look* mean. Their faces even showed a bit of sympathy. Sympathy! I think that was the worst thing of all. "Yeah," I said. "I guess."

"Oh, well," Kristy said, looking at her watch. "See you at lunch."

" 'Bye," I said.

" 'Bye," the other three said.

I felt awful as I watched them walk off. It was as if they had taken my heart out and stepped all over it.

"They're nuts," Logan whispered. "I think they're just jealous."

I didn't believe that for a minute. Maybe all those people in the hallway had been lying to me, just trying to make me feel good. "Logan, do you *really* like my hair?"

Logan held my shoulders gently and looked me in the eye. "I *really* do. But that shouldn't matter. Mary Anne, you don't need to listen to what anyone says. *You're* the one who has to like it. If it makes you feel good, that's what counts."

Leave it to Logan. He was right. I liked the way it looked, I liked the way it felt. "Yeah," I said. "Thanks."

"Okay, I better go before the bell rings. 'Bye."

" 'Bye!" As he turned to leave, I saw Dawn sitting in homeroom. She caught my eye, then looked away.

Suddenly I remembered the BSC meeting that afternoon. "Oh — Logan?" I called down the hall.

"Yeah?" he said, turning back around.

"Are you coming to the meeting?"

"I hadn't planned on it. Why? You want me to?"

How did he know? I smiled and nodded. "I don't think I can face it alone. You know . . ."

"Okay!" he said. "Anyway, I'll see you at lunch. 'Bye!"

" 'Bye!"

I walked in the classroom. I could tell right away that Dawn had heard me. She was shaking her head and staring out the window, with a teeny little smirk on her face.

CHAPTER 8

Wenesday

Well, it was my turn with the twines. What with the lovly whether outside, Litle miss Mot moteart moztar Baitoven at the piano, and the mad Sient Sceintist downstairs, it loked like it was gonna be a long evning. (Oh, by the way, Im still confusd about this time travel buzness. Does anybody understand the prixsip principals? Pleas someone give me a lessen, in very easy terms my brane can take.

Where was I? Oh, yeah. Anyway, thanks to Stacy, things got a litle livlier ...

The weather report had predicted heavy snow for Tuesday. They were right about the heavy part, but they were wrong about the snow. Freezing rain fell the whole day long. No matter how hard you tried, you couldn't feel warm or dry — inside or out.

So there was Claudia, inside the Arnolds' kitchen, cold and bored silly. Marilyn was practicing scales over and over, Carolyn was still working on her contraption, and the last drizzlings of the storm tapped against the windows.

After listening to the clanking downstairs, Claudia was getting curious. She went to the top of the basement stairs and shouted, "Do you want something to eat?"

"No!" Carolyn shouted back.

"I can bring it down."

"*No!*"

"Can't I just come down?"

"NO! I told you this is top secret!"

Claudia rolled her eyes. "But you let Mary Anne and Marilyn see it a few days ago."

"I wasn't working on the secret stuff back then! Please leave me alone!"

"All right."

Claudia slunk back to the kitchen table. In her shoulder bag was a Nancy Drew book she'd just finished reading. With a sigh, she pulled it out and started reading it again.

By the end of the first chapter, Marilyn finished practicing. She bounced into the kitchen and said, "Let's go see the time machine!"

"*Noooooo!*" Carolyn screamed from the basement.

"I think she means no," Claudia said.

"What a party pooper," Marilyn replied with a pout. "I know, let's invite someone over!"

Good idea, Claudia thought. Stacey was sitting at the Braddocks', just a couple of blocks away. "We could try Matt and Haley," she said. "I don't know if Stacey'll want to take them out in this weather, though."

"The rain's almost stopped!" Marilyn squealed. "Call them up!"

It turned out that Stacey was happy to bring the kids over. In a few minutes she and the Braddocks appeared at the door, soggy but excited.

"Hi!" Haley and Stacey shouted.

"Hi!" Marilyn replied. "Come in!"

Matt beamed and made a motion with his hand. A small, low noise came from his mouth. (Matt has been deaf since birth. He goes to a special school in Stamford, and speaks with sign language. I haven't caught on how to do that, but Jessi's really good at it.)

They hung their coats in the closet and came into the kitchen.

"Don't let them downstairs!" Carolyn's voice floated upward.

"What?" Marilyn said in an exaggerated loud voice. *"Let them come downstairs?* Okay! Let's go, guys!"

"No!" Carolyn shrieked. "Don't! I said *don't!"*

Marilyn giggled. "Come on," she said to her friends. "Let's play."

The three of them ran into the rec room.

Stacey and Claudia went into the living room, flopped onto the sofa, and gabbed for awhile. (Claudia didn't mention what they were gabbing about, and I didn't ask, but I have a pretty good idea. . . .)

Well, the topic must have been *very* interesting (harrumph), because they lost track of the kids.

"Claudia?" Stacey said. "Do you hear anything?"

Claud sat up. "No."

"That's what I was afraid of. What are they doing?" Stacey stood up and headed out of the living room.

She stopped when she heard scurrying footsteps outside. "Why are they — "

There was a burst of giggling from the side of the house. Stacey and Claudia looked out the window to see Marilyn, Matt, and Haley, with their coats on, running down the driveway.

"Come on," Claudia said. She dashed to the closet, grabbed their coats, and called down to let Carolyn know they were going outside. Then she and Stacey bundled up and left through the back door.

The rain had stopped, but it was still freezing. Claud and Stace walked around the side of the house, looking for the kids.

They found them on their knees, peering through a small basement window. Haley signed something to Matt, and he laughed.

I should explain, Matt's laugh is . . . well, unusual. It's sort of a cross between a loud squeak and a goose's honk. (He can't help it, he's never heard what it sounds like!) Anyway, it made Marilyn crack up. Haley thought it was pretty funny, too. As for Matt, I think he likes the way his laugh affects people. Their reaction makes him laugh even more.

But Carolyn had heard it, too, and she had a different opinion. "Knock it off!" she called from the basement. "Get away from there!"

The three spies raced away. They saw Claudia and Stacey, but they ignored them. They headed for the green slanted door that led into the basement from outside.

"Ssssshhh!" Marilyn warned. She gently pulled the door open.

Eeeeeeeeee.

The kids cracked up again at the squeaky hinge.

"Hey!" came Carolyn's voice.

Marilyn let the door fall open. She and the others stepped back and stared as Carolyn angrily stomped up the stairs. She poked her head out and reached for the door handle.

On her face was a snorkel mask, complete with pipe. A pair of fluffy earmuffs was on her head, and a big wool scarf around her neck. Between the mask and the muffs, her hair was sticking out every which way.

Claudia had to admit, she looked ridiculous.

The kids thought so, too. They screamed with laughter.

"Go away!" Carolyn yelled. "You're ruining my concentration! Claudia, get them out of here!"

She disappeared back into the basement, slamming the door behind her.

"Come on, guys," Claud said. "Let's go inside."

The kids ran in the back door ahead of Claudia and Stacey. "And stay away from the basement steps!" Stacey warned them.

The kids settled down. They spent the rest

of the time in the rec room. Claud and Stace set up a game of Mousetrap, which held their attention just fine.

Every once in awhile they could hear a bang or a bonk or a boing from downstairs. But they had lost interest in the time machine by then.

Until Carolyn herself suddenly barged into the rec room. Her eyes were practically on fire. She was wearing the same crazy outfit, without the mask. A ratty old wool hat was now perched above the earmuffs. Claudia said she looked positively demented.

"Eureka!" she shouted.

"Eureka?" repeated Claudia.

Haley looked puzzled. "You need a vacuum cleaner?"

"No," Carolyn said. "I've solved the final mystery. The last obstacle to time travel!"

"Uh-huh," Marilyn replied. "What happened? You rearranged the milk crates?"

Carolyn ignored that remark. "Soon," she said, grinning wildly, "I will be ready for my first flight!"

There was something arresting about the look in her eyes. No one was sassing her now. Claudia said a shiver ran down her spine.

She almost believed Carolyn.

CHAPTER 9

I had learned a new word. *Pariah.*

It sounds like an exotic name, but it's not. It means "outcast." I had come across it in a newspaper, then looked it up. Funny how it seemed to fit me these days.

I found one good thing about being a pariah. I got to eat lunch with Logan, *alone.*

That's right. My friends, the supposedly truest friends of my whole life, the girls I'd shared everything with, were eating at another table.

And probably talking about me.

To be completely honest, it was I who decided not to eat with them. You see, they hadn't said a single nice thing to me since I had gotten the makeover, and it was already Thursday. Monday's club meeting had been torture. If Logan hadn't been there, I think I would have jumped out the window. Of course, I made Logan come to Wednesday's, too. But that one was even worse. I had decided to wear the casual outfit I'd bought at Steven E, and the snide comments were flying.

To add insult to injury, now the members of the BSC were spreading crazy rumors about me around the school. Rumors that some high school guy liked me. Can you believe it?

Well, I had had enough. Their attitude was stupid and mean. And that's exactly what I was explaining to Logan at lunch.

"What rumors?" Logan asked.

"You don't want to hear," I said.

"Who's spreading them?"

"Logan, I'm not going to talk about it. It's not worth it."

"But it's upsetting you. So why don't you tell me? You'll probably feel better."

I took a tasteless bite of Salisbury steak and thought about how to word my reply. "Well, it's just that . . . supposedly there's this friend of Kristy's brother Sam, named Chris Something, who . . . well, who said I was cute, and wanted to know my name."

There. I had said it.

Logan looked at me blankly. "So what?" He shrugged. "What's the big deal? I don't understand."

"That doesn't bother you?"

"No. I mean, I'm not surprised." Logan's

eyes crinkled as he flashed that famous smile. "If I were him, I'd ask the same thing."

"It's just that they're talking about me behind my back, that's all," I said. "And they're talking about me to other people."

"Mary Anne, maybe you're taking this a little too seriously."

"Logan, it's true. Sometimes I catch people looking at me, and when I look back they glance away. And I can hear all these muttered comments when I walk down the hall. It's so immature. I can't stand it!"

"Maybe you should sit down and have a talk with your friends," Logan suggested.

"I thought about that, but you know what? I feel disgusted, Logan. I'm supposed to go shopping with Kristy this afternoon to buy art supplies for our Kid-Kits, and I don't even want to go."

"But Kristy would listen to you. She's your best friend."

"She *was*. Who do you think started spreading the rumors?"

Logan nodded. "Yeah . . . well, it's sad. Maybe you do need to cool off."

"What are you doing after school?"

"Um, I'm supposed to go to Austin's around five-thirty, but nothing before then. Want to come over?"

"Okay!" Spending the afternoon at the Brunos' would be a much better idea than shopping with Kristy the Gossip.

I saw Kristy in the hallway before last period. I really had to force myself to look her in the eye. "I'm not going to be able to go with you this afternoon," I said.

"Oh." She didn't seem crushed, but I could tell she wasn't overjoyed, either. "Well, I guess I can find enough stuff myself."

"Okay," I said.

"Will you be at the meeting?" Kristy asked.

"Yeah."

"See you."

" 'Bye."

It was mid-winter, but it felt chillier inside than out.

After school, I met Logan and we walked to his house. As soon as we stepped through the door, Logan's brother and sister ran into the living room to see us. Hunter jumped up and down, pointing to my head. "Your hair! Your hair! Your hair!" he cried out. "I like it!"

Kerry was staring at me in awe. "You look so *grown-up*, Mary Anne."

"Thanks," I said.

Hunter and Kerry are adorable, and it was nice to see them so excited and hear their compliments. A couple of days before I would have loved it. But I was tired of drawing attention to myself. I kind of wished I had an Old Mary Anne wig I could put on for awhile.

Logan and I were making hot chocolate in the kitchen, when I brought up something that was bothering me. "Um, you're going to Austin's house today?"

"Yeah," Logan said. "He came over for dinner once last week, and his parents invited me to his house."

"Oh. So you definitely can't come to the BSC meeting?"

"Sorry. But you can handle it, Mary Anne."

"I guess." I sighed. "But a half *hour* of the cold shoulder?"

"Bring something to read," Logan suggested. "That'll fill up the silence."

"Yeah, but what if they start making comments again? Then what should I do?"

Logan frowned and stirred his cocoa. "Well, let's work out a plan. What could happen?"

"They could say something about my hair."

"Tell them you feel great. Tell them *they* should try it. What else?"

"They could tell me my outfit is ugly or it doesn't fit right."

"Well, they're *wrong*, you know that. So you can just say, like, 'That's funny. It was one of the nicest outfits I saw there. And everyone seems to like it but you.' Something like that. Remember, *you* like the way you look." He quickly added, "I mean, I do, too, and so do a lot of other people, but you're the important one."

As you can see, Logan is very take-charge. (And he knows how it feels when people talk behind his back. Once, he had to become a regular BSC member when Dawn went to Los Angeles for a few weeks — and when his football teammates found out, they were awful to him.)

We talked and talked, and by the end of our conversation, I felt prepared for anything. At about five-fifteen, we put on our coats and left the house. Austin's is the opposite direction from Claudia's, so we said good-bye on the front lawn.

Out of the corner of my eye, I noticed a familiar car drive by. Charlie was taking Kristy to the meeting.

"Uh-oh," I said.

"They didn't stop to pick you up," Logan remarked.

"That doesn't surprise me. But I told Kristy I couldn't go shopping with her, remember? And now here I am."

"Where did you say you were going to be?"

I shrugged. "She didn't ask why I couldn't come."

"Then don't worry about it. It's your business."

"Yeah. Okay, see you tomorrow."

" 'Bye."

We gave each other little good-bye kisses and left.

Boy, was there a chilly breeze in Claudia's room when I got there. It came from Kristy and Stacey and Dawn and Claudia (especially Kristy), and it blasted me from head to toe.

But I knew just what to do. I said "Hi," took the record book, sat down on the bed, and did my work.

No one said a word to me. I tried to be strong. But I have to say, when the phone rang I felt a shiver of relief.

"Hello, Baby-sitters Club," Claudia said into the receiver. "Hi, Mrs. P! Uh-huh. Okay, hold on, let me check." She covered the receiver and looked at me. "A week from this Thursday, six to ten."

I looked at the calendar. Jessi and Mallory can't sit at night, Kristy was sitting for the Arnolds, and Claudia was going out with her family. Dawn and Stacey were free, but they had heavy sitting schedules the rest of the week.

"I could do it," I volunteered.

As Claudia confirmed the date with Mrs.

Prezzioso, Kristy gave me a sidelong glance. "You sure?"

"Yeah. Why?"

"What if Logan wants to go out?"

I shrugged. "We'll just — "

"I mean, there are *some* people who give up their girlfriends for the sake of their boyfriends . . ." Kristy let a silence hang in the air, then looked around and said, "Want to see what I bought for the Kid-Kits today?"

"Yeah!" everyone said. They leaned forward as Kristy brought out a paper bag crammed with stuff.

Me? I just sat there, speechless. I thought I'd prepared myself for every mean comment. I never expected that one.

What else would they think of? When was this going to end?

I was determined not to cry. I looked down at the record book. The names started to blur. And for the first time, I had the terrible feeling that this was all wrong. From the start.

Maybe I just didn't belong in the Baby-sitters Club.

CHAPTER 10

"Does it come in other colors, too?" Hannah Toce asked, admiring my cable-knit sweater.

"Uh-huh," I replied. "But once they sell out, they'll only have spring clothes, so you should probably go there soon."

"Okay, thanks, Mary Anne!" she said, turning to look for an empty seat in the study hall. "Oh," she added, "and good luck with that guy."

"What guy?"

"I heard a high school guy liked you. Is that . . . off?"

"Um, no. I mean, yes!" I laughed. "I mean, it's only a rumor."

Hannah bit her lower lip in embarrassment. "Oh. Sorry."

"It's okay," I said.

"Well, 'bye." She walked away, toward a table near the window.

I couldn't stop smiling. It was Monday, almost a week since that rumor started. I'd kind of forgotten about it. Now that I'd been reminded, I felt a little different than I had before. Although I'd never admit it to Logan (or Kristy), I was *flattered* to think that some unknown tenth-grader was pining away for little old me.

You see, something unexpected had happened because of my New Look. I was getting to know all these girls I had only vaguely known before, plus some others, like Hannah, I'd never met at all. She'd always seemed so glamorous and popular and aloof. Now I was discovering that she wasn't aloof at all.

And Hannah wasn't the only one. Sabrina Bouvier and Susan Taylor, for instance, were two girls the BSC never liked. Why? Because they wore lots of makeup and expensive clothes, and seemed snobby. Well, *seemed* is the important word. It turned out that Sabrina and Susan were really friendly. On Friday they had complimented me on something, out of the blue.

I was beginning to realize that snobbery can go two ways. Maybe it was the BSC members who were sticking *their* noses up at other girls, just because of the way the girls looked.

After all, that's what they were doing to me.

After Kristy's nasty comment at Friday's meeting, I made a vow to myself. No, I wasn't going to quit the club (although I had thought about it). Instead, I decided this: I would honor all my sitting jobs, but I wasn't going to go to another meeting until someone apologized to me. Or at least said something nice.

Just thinking about the BSC was enough to upset me. As long as I kept my mind off the club members, I felt pretty good. Looking around during study hall, I could see Sabrina a couple of tables away. Our eyes met, and I smiled. I could tell by the look in her eyes that she wanted to say something, but a teacher was pacing the floor beside her. So she just smiled back and glanced down at her work.

I sneaked the compact out from my purse and checked my makeup. Funny, I always thought that was so *tacky* when other girls did it, but there was really no other convenient way. Besides, I was very quick about it.

And the makeup still looked fine.

I opened the book *A Separate Peace*, which was my English assignment (I may have been the New Mary Anne, but I still had the Old Study Habits). But it was about these boys in some boarding school, and I was having a hard time keeping my eyes on the page.

Before I knew it, Sabrina was pulling up a chair next to me. "So is it true about Carlos?" she whispered.

Now, Sabrina had told me she was a soap

opera fan. So at first I thought she might be talking about some soap character. I had this image of a TV screen with credits rolling by and an announcer saying, "Today . . . the Truth About Carlos!"

"Um, I don't know," I said. "Who's Carlos?"

She looked flabbergasted. "Carlos *Mendez*. You know."

I thought for a moment, trying to place the name. Then I shook my head. "Nope."

Sabrina rolled her eyes. She grinned mischievously. "You haven't heard? It figures, the one person who *should* know, doesn't!" She laughed, as if that were the most hilarious thought in the world.

This was getting ridiculous. "Well?"

Sabrina leaned forward. "He's only one of the hunkiest guys in the high school. And everyone's saying that he invited you to the Winter Dance."

"Well . . . he didn't," I replied. "And I don't even know about the Winter Dance. Is it different than the January Jamboree?"

"Yes," Sabrina said. "You're going to that with *Logan*." She narrowed her eyes. "You are, aren't you?"

"Yes!"

"The Winter Dance is at SHS, for the *high*

school students." She sighed. "It's always so much fun."

Always? She sounded as if she'd been going to it since she was a toddler. "Anyway," she continued, "maybe it's just a rumor. Or maybe he hasn't gotten up the nerve to call yet."

Now I really wanted to laugh. "We'll see, I guess," I said.

"Let me know what happens," Sabrina whispered. And she scooted back to her table.

Honestly, I didn't know what to make of that. The idea was absurd. But who knew? Maybe my life was about to change. Maybe I really was going to learn the Truth About Carlos.

No, no, no. I didn't *honestly* feel that way. Nobody was about to take me away from Logan. I mean, it was fun to think that yet another older boy liked me, but I'm definitely a one-boy girl.

Still, I felt uncomfortable when I saw Logan at lunch later on. Just the thought of these two phantom guys made me a little uneasy around him. I wanted to talk about them, but I couldn't.

My dad once told me that a rumor hurts three people: the person whom the rumor's about, the person who tells it, and the person who hears it. What if the rumor was really a lie? What if Carlos (or Chris) didn't know about me at all? Why involve Logan? He'd say it was no big deal, but he might not mean it.

So lunchtime was not exactly carefree. There I was, ignoring my best friends because they hated me, and keeping secrets from the only person I felt close to. Fortunately, Logan didn't seem to notice anything was wrong.

We managed to avoid the subject of the BSC for a record amount of time. But eventually Logan asked, "Anybody call a truce yet?"

I shook my head. "We're still not talking."

"Not even with Dawn? How do you manage that?"

"It's a big house."

Logan speared some spaghetti and twirled it around. "I don't know, Mary Anne. Something's got to give."

"Yeah, but they're all acting so awful. And you know what? I just can't face them another time, Logan. Friday was torture. I'm not going back until they're nice to me."

"Not going to the meetings? Isn't that a little extreme? I mean, this is getting out of hand. I can feel the tension myself."

I shrugged and fiddled with my food. "Well, maybe I'll reconsider."

I did reconsider, but each time I made up my mind to face my "friends," I got cold feet. To begin with, I'm terrible at confrontations.

I always tremble like a leaf — and that's when it's one on one. The idea of going up against all the members of the BSC was terrifying.

I was still reconsidering at five-fifteen that afternoon. I was in my room, trying to decide whether to grab my down coat or stay put. Dawn was home, too. Usually, if we're both here, we leave together. The past few meetings, we'd managed to avoid each other because of after-school activities or other commitments that kept us out of the house.

I was sort of hoping Dawn would knock on my door and make a peace offering. We could cry, laugh, make up, then walk to the meeting together. All would be forgiven and forgotten.

When I heard the front door slam, I ran to my window and looked out.

There was Dawn, hands in pockets and head bent to the ground. She was walking quickly in the direction of Claudia's house, her breath making little cotton puffs in the frigid cold.

I stared at her for awhile. Then I went to my desk and began a long homework assignment.

An hour later, Sharon poked her head in my room. "Oh. Mary Anne! When did you get back?"

"I've been here all along," I replied.

She scratched her head. "Is it Tuesday already? I thought — "

"No, it's Monday. I — stayed home."

I was trying to figure out what excuse to make when Dawn's voice shouted from downstairs. "I'm ho-ome! Anybody here?"

"Excuse me," Sharon said. She went to the stairs and shouted, "I'll be right down!"

Then she turned back into my room and said, "Mary Anne, have you seen the spaghetti tongs?"

"They're on the towels in the linen closet," I told her.

"Oh. Thanks."

(You get used to that kind of thing in this house.)

Sharon left, and I got ready for dinner.

I didn't feel too bad. I really thought that staying home from the meeting had relieved pressure. I figured the distance was good for me.

What I didn't figure was that I'd be eating dinner with the Stepsister from the Black Lagoon.

"Hi," I said as I ran downstairs to set the table for dinner.

"Hello, beautiful," said Dad, peeking out from the kitchen.

"Hope you're hungry," added Sharon cheerfully.

Nothing, said Dawn.

I went into the kitchen to get plates, napkins, and utensils. Dad had this gleam in his eye. "I brought home a special treat tonight."

"More clothes for Mary Anne?" Dawn called in from the dining room.

Fire One.

"Nope," Dad said. "Four different dishes from a new Thai restaurant that opened near work. I asked the chef to give me the best — meatless, of course."

"Yum!" I said as I carried everything to the table.

"Oh, is Mary Anne eating with us tonight?" Dawn asked her mom, as if I weren't in the room.

Sharon looked confused. (I think she and Dad knew *exactly* what was going on, but they were trying to let us fight our own battle.) "Yes, Dawn," she said.

"Oh," Dawn replied nonchalantly. "I thought maybe she was going to Logan's."

Fire Two.

I did not answer. I just set the table and took my seat. Calmly.

"Mmmm, smell that coconut sauce!" Dad said, taking the lid off a food tin.

"I'm starving," Sharon put in.

"Me, too," I said.

"You should be," Dawn said. "You missed all your favorite junk food."

That was enough. I pushed back my chair and stood up. "Excuse me, please."

Fighting back tears, I ran upstairs to be alone.

CHAPTER 11

"Will you listen to this piece?" Marilyn Arnold asked. "Please, just once? So I can feel what it's like to *perform* it in front of someone?"

Carolyn burst into the living room, wearing a down parka. "I'm going outside," she announced.

"I wasn't asking *you!*" Marilyn snapped.

"I wasn't *answering* you!" Carolyn shot back.

It was Saturday afternoon, and I was sitting for the twins again. Since I hadn't gone to meetings all week Kristy had actually called me to ask if I was still going to take the job. She didn't apologize, didn't ask why I hadn't shown up at the meetings, didn't even yell at me. Just, "Hi. Should we send someone else to the Arnolds'?" I said, "No, I'll go," and that was the end of the conversation.

I may have been having problems with the Baby-sitters Club, but I still liked baby-sitting.

Marilyn was practicing for a big recital. I had

no idea *what* Carolyn was doing. "Okay, one at a time, please," I said. "Yes, Marilyn, I'd love to listen. And you can go outside, Carolyn. Do you have your gloves and hat?"

"It's warm out today!" Carolyn insisted.

She was right — sort of. The temperature had gone up to the low forties, which felt like midsummer after the cold spell. "Well, take them along, just in case," I said. "And don't go too far. If you decide to play at a friend's house, let me know. Okay?"

"Uh-huh. 'Bye!"

" 'Bye!"

As she ran out the front door, Marilyn said, "Sit on the sofa and pretend you're the audience."

"Okay." I sat down and smiled.

Marilyn stood stiffly by the piano. In a barely audible voice, she mumbled, "Thefopeeisfrayoasebabaswelltenklavy," and quick sat down.

"Huh?" I said.

"I was just introducing the piece," Marilyn replied. "The teacher makes us do that."

"But I couldn't understand what you said. Don't forget, the introduction is part of the recital. People will want to know what you're playing. Can you speak more clearly?"

Marilyn exhaled impatiently and pulled herself to her feet. "The following piece is from

Johann Sebastian Bach's 'The Well-Tempered Clavichord,' " she said in a monotone. "Okay?"

"Much better," I said, applauding enthusiastically.

Marilyn played away. I'm not much of a musician, but I thought she sounded pretty good. I heard a couple of clinkers, but everybody makes mistakes. Anyway, I sure couldn't have done better. I cheered at the end.

"Encore! Encore! That was great!"

Marilyn giggled. "Mary Anne, that stunk."

"Stank," I said. "That *stank*."

Her face fell. "It did?"

"No! I meant, you were using the wrong word. When you said, 'stunk,' you meant 'stank.' It's like, 'it *stinks*, it *stank*, it has *stunk*' — you know, like *sink, sank, sunk*."

"Huh?"

My explanation stank. And I was sunk.

"Never mind," I said. "You sounded great! I think you have nothing to worry about."

"Well, I need to work on the fingerings. I'm going to practice some more. Will you listen to me later on?"

"Sure."

"Thanks."

Marilyn began playing again, and I went into the kitchen. I had brought *A Separate Peace* with me, and I started reading.

It seemed as if only a few minutes had gone by when Marilyn came into the kitchen. "I'm ready," she said. "Want to listen?"

"Sure." I put down my book and looked at the clock. Almost an hour had passed. In the back of my mind, I began wondering where Carolyn was.

Marilyn announced her piece, *much* more clearly than before. And even I noticed how much better she played it. I clapped wildly.

She sprang up from her seat, beaming. "That didn't stink, did it?"

"No way!" I said. "Even Bach couldn't have done better."

"Thanks."

I looked out the living room window, thinking about Carolyn again. "What do you say we go look for your sister?"

"Okay," Marilyn said.

We put on our coats and went outside. It didn't take us long to track down Carolyn. She was down the street, standing with a clipboard on someone's front lawn. Eight or nine kids were gathered around her.

"Time?" she asked one of them.

He shrugged. "I can't tell time."

Carolyn exhaled. "Haven't you been *listening*? I want you to tell me what time you want to travel to in my time machine — you know, like to ancient Greece, or to the year you were born, or to the future . . ."

"I want to go to now!" one kid blurted out. "*Dzzzzzit!* Hey, it worked!" He laughed loudly.

I guess there's an Alan Gray in every bunch.

"This is serious!" Carolyn insisted. "The first flight leaves on Thursday night, at the full moon. Be there or be square." She turned to the nearest girl, pencil in hand, and asked again, "Time?"

"Um . . . when my grandma was a girl," she said.

"Can you be more exact? Say, 1930?"

"Okay."

"Place?" Carolyn asked.

"Brooklyn," the girl answered. "That's where she grew up."

Carolyn scribbled furiously on a legal pad that was attached to the clipboard. "That'll be one dollar, in today's currency."

The girl dug into her jeans pocket. "That's expensive," she muttered.

"It would buy a lot in 1930," Carolyn said. "Things were much cheaper then. Think of it that way."

"Me next!" a boy shouted.

"Time?" Carolyn asked.

Marilyn shook her head. "What is she *doing*?"

"Taking reservations for her time machine," I replied.

"Does she really believe that thing works?"

It was a good question. If she did, she was going to be in for a big shock. And so were all the kids who had paid her money.

If she didn't, then she was cheating them.

I didn't know what to do. I stood there like a fool, watching Carolyn scribble away and rob those poor kids. Her pocket was stuffed with dollar bills and the kids seemed awfully excited.

Kristy came to mind. She was so practical about things like this. So was Stacey. What would they do?

Normally I would have called them and asked their advice. But I couldn't do that now. Not while I was a BSC pariah.

I thought I'd managed to go a whole day without feeling frustrated and upset about the Baby-sitters Club.

I was wrong.

CHAPTER 12

I thought Sabrina was going to burst. Her eyes were wide open and her fingers were clenching and unclenching her books. "So?" she asked.

I stuffed my book in my locker. "So?" I repeated.

"So . . . wasn't I right?"

"Right about what?"

"Carlos!"

"Oh, *Carlos*!"

"So he *did* call you — and you're going, right? Oh, I *knew* it! You are soooo lucky!"

"Wait, wait!" I protested. "Sabrina, I don't know what you're talking about."

"Mary Anne," said Sabrina seriously, "are you trying to make fun of me? Because if you are — "

"Oh, no!" I said.

"I mean, it's all over school. You accepted

Carlos's invitation. It's a little silly to try to keep it from *me* when — "

"Um, Sabrina, I'm supposed to see a teacher before lunch. I'll — I'll talk to you later, okay?" I hated lying like that, but this conversation was completely dumb. I wanted to put an end to it.

"If you say so," Sabrina replied with a shrug. "Bye."

" 'Bye."

I walked through the maze of hallways, pretending to head to a classroom.

Imagine! The week before, Carlos had asked me to the dance. This week, I had accepted. I supposed next week we'd be engaged. What a story.

But it was no longer amusing. And I was having second thoughts about Sabrina as a friend.

After awhile I turned around and walked to the cafeteria. I wasn't going to let this silly rumor upset me. There was too much else on my mind.

For one thing, it was Monday, and I was about to see my ex-friends for the first time since Friday. Once again I'd go through the daily ritual: Pretend not to notice them, try not to be depressed that they weren't noticing me, stick with Logan.

For another, I was still confused about Carolyn Arnold's scam and what I should do about it. Also, I was starting to think about the BSC record book, whether the other girls were keeping it up properly. I was sort of insulted they hadn't come crying to me about how difficult it was to fill my shoes.

Carlos was not on the top of my worry list.

I sat in my usual spot at the opposite end of the cafeteria from the BSC table. I could see Claudia and Stacey laughing hysterically about something as Dawn sat down next to them.

They looked so happy. And I felt as if I were exiled in Siberia.

Well, it didn't matter. As soon as Logan arrived, I'd feel less lonely. I looked toward the lunch line and then the door, but he wasn't either place. I wondered if he had a math test in the afternoon. When he does, sometimes he takes a study hall at lunch.

I dug into my Chicken Kiev. (Do you ever wonder how they come up with these names? I guess if they called it "Unidentified Leftover Gristle with Lumpy Brown Sauce," no one would go near it.) As usual, it tasted like burned flour over rubber bands. But I managed to eat most of it and get the taste out of my mouth with some salad.

I kept glancing around for Logan. By the time I finished eating, he hadn't showed up. Bored out of my mind, I stood up to return my tray. I figured I'd spend the rest of the lunch period in the library. At least it would be peaceful, and away from the BSC members. And maybe Logan was there, cramming. It would be nice to see him, even if he was busy.

I looked up to find Susan Taylor walking toward me. "Mary Anne? What are you doing here all alone? You want to come sit at our table?"

I thought about it for a moment. She was nice to ask, but I saw Sabrina at the table and I didn't want to talk about silly rumors. "Thanks," I said, "but I'm going to the library and I'm sort of late."

"Late for the library?"

"I'm . . . meeting someone there." (Well, I *might* have been. It wasn't a total lie.)

"Okay, maybe tomorrow. 'Bye."

" 'Bye."

I returned my tray, took one last look around for Logan, and left.

I went upstairs to the library, which was pretty crowded. A group of kids was huddled over some encyclopedias at one table. Two boys were leafing through the humongous dictionary on the pedestal, pointing out words and giggling (on Dirty-Word Patrol, Kristy used to say). I found two empty chairs together at a table near the window.

Before doing any work, I took a stroll

through the stacks of books. I started at the sports books and worked my way around the room.

Logan was nowhere to be seen.

I wasn't too upset. He was probably having a conference with a teacher, or he might have gotten roped into a game of touch football with some friends. Still, it would have been nice to see him.

With a sigh, I sat down to begin some homework. I set my bookbag on the seat next to me, so no one would sit there. Just in case.

Logan didn't show up in the library. In fact, I didn't see him the rest of the day. I wondered if he had even come to school. Maybe he was sick, poor thing.

After last period, on the way to my locker, I passed by the boys' gym. The doors were open and I could hear the frantic squeaking of sneakers on the polished floor. "Foul!" shouted a familiar voice.

I peeked inside to see Logan playing basketball with a bunch of guys. Trevor Sandbourne was one of them, and he saw me out of the corner of his eye. He gave me a very small wave, then snapped his attention back to the game. Logan was standing under the basket, facing away from me. He held the basketball over his head, waiting to pass it as the other boys ran around like crazy.

I didn't want to interrupt him or embarrass him, so I ducked back into the hallway. At least I knew he wasn't sick at home.

But why hadn't he looked for me all day? Hmmmm.

I put it out of my mind. I'd call him before dinner. After all, I'd have plenty of time, since I wasn't going to the BSC meeting.

I was feeling tired and confused. All I wanted to do was go home and curl up on my bed.

So I did. Tigger purred and tucked himself into me. I petted him, but I felt distracted. I tried not to think about the meeting. Obviously the other girls were doing fine without me. I tried not to think about Logan. As for Carolyn, well, I figured I might as well enjoy my last few days before being thrown in jail for aiding and abetting an extortion scheme. My life was a mess.

At least I had a nice haircut.

I read for awhile in bed, then ended up taking a little nap. I dreamed I was trapped in a castle tower by an evil king and queen (who were Kristy and Dawn). As I looked out the tower window, I saw Logan below. He was tossing a basketball into a hoop on the castle wall. "Can you save me?" I called down.

"Sure," he said casually. "Let down your hair."

Oops.

I awoke to the ringing of the phone. I sat up and looked at my clock. It was eleven after six.

"Mary Anne?" called Sharon's voice from downstairs. "It's Logan!"

Yea! I ran out of my room and into my parents' room. Grabbing the phone, I said, "Hulluhhh . . ."

My throat was thick from the nap. I quickly cleared it and giggled. "I mean, hello!"

Logan didn't laugh. "Hi," he said softly.

"I didn't see you today," I said.

"Trevor said you looked in at our game."

"Yeah, but I didn't want to bother you."

"Uh-huh."

"You guys were playing hard . . ."

"Yeah. Good game."

His voice drifted off. I knew something was wrong, but I was afraid to ask what. The last thing I needed was a fight with Logan. But why was he mad? What could this possibly be about?

"Um, Mary Anne?" Logan finally said. "I called because I wanted to ask you something. I mean, you know, we had this date for the January Jamboree, and we hadn't really talked much about it . . ."

Oh, no. He was going to go to the dance with someone else. I swallowed a lump in my throat.

"So," he continued, "I, uh, just wanted to, um, confirm . . . are we still going?"

Huh?

"I — don't know," I said. *"Are* we still going?"

"Well, I need to know, Mary Anne. Because if you don't want to go with me — "

"Don't want to go with you?" I thought I was hearing things — or maybe still dreaming. "What do you mean? Do you want to go with *me*?"

There was a silence on the other end. I heard Logan take a deep breath. "Look, Mary Anne, I don't know how to say this, but . . . well, I know all about your other . . . your other . . ."

I sank down on my parents' bed in shock. "Carlos," I murmured under my breath.

"Yeah," Logan said. "I know about Carlos. And the Winter Dance. And — "

"But Logan," I interrupted, "he's not — "

"You don't need to explain, Mary Anne. Really. We're not . . . married or anything. You have every right. I mean, I admit I'm . . . *surprised*. I wish you had mentioned something to me. I would have felt better if I had known up front, but, well, I know you have trouble with confrontations. I just think you should let me know now about the Jamboree, so — "

"Oh, boy," I said, shaking my head. "Do we need to talk."

"Yeah, I think we do."

Poor Logan sounded as if he were trying as hard as he could to keep from sounding hurt — or furious.

I drew in a deep breath. "Logan, what you were hearing was just a stupid rumor. Some girls got it in their heads that this guy, Carlos, was interested in me. They made up a story about how he asked me to the dance and I said yes. The truth is, I don't even know what he looks like."

"Really?"

"Really."

"Then . . . then why would they say a thing like that if it weren't true?"

"I don't know! That's what *I've* been wondering!"

"And why didn't you tell me?"

"I wanted to! I just thought it might make you upset. Besides, it seemed so silly, and *talking* about it would have made it more important than it was. I don't know. I figured if I just avoided it, it would blow over."

"Right . . ." I could imagine Logan nodding, his brow crinkled. "I guess you've been avoiding a lot of things lately."

"Yeah," I said. "And none of them has blown over." I started to cry. Logan was right. For the last few weeks, I'd been keeping so much inside. I felt like a big dam, swollen with water and about to burst.

"Mary Anne," Logan said. "I believe you. I just want you to know that."

"Thanks," I said.

"And don't worry about the rumor. If you want to keep quiet about it, that's okay. I mean, everyone will see it's wrong eventually, right?"

"No," I said, sniffling back some tears. "No. I'm tired of keeping quiet, Logan. I'm going to sit down with Sabrina *and* her friends tomorrow and set them straight."

"That's a good idea."

"I'm really sorry. I didn't mean to upset you."

"Hey, I can take it," Logan said. "Now I don't have to go hang out at the high school playground tomorrow."

"Huh?"

"You know, to check out Carlos, see what makes him so special."

"Well," I said, "if you do decide to go, tell him I turn down his offer."

"Aha! I knew it!"

"Go eat your dinner," I said, laughing.

"Okay. 'Bye, Mary Anne," Logan replied. "See you tomorrow."

" 'Bye!"

I hung up the phone, feeling great. I was glad we had talked about our problem before it got out of hand.

When I turned around, Dawn was standing in the doorway.

"Talking to Logan *again*?" she said. "Or was that Carlos?" With a look of scorn, she turned around and left.

Okay, I thought to myself. This has gone far enough.

CHAPTER 13

"Dawn?" I called out.

No answer.

"Dawn?"

I could hear her footsteps on the stairs. I ran to the top of the stairwell. "Dawn, did you hear me?"

Dawn was practically at the bottom before she turned around. This look of make-believe shock was on her face. "Are you calling *me*?"

"I don't know any other Dawn in the house."

Whoa. I couldn't believe I said that.

I don't think Dawn believed it, either. She did a double take.

I tried to smile. The idea was to have a discussion, not an argument. "Can we talk?" I asked.

"What a surprise," Dawn said. "I didn't think you were talking to me."

"I didn't think you were talking to *me*!"

Dawn gave me a withering look. "I'm not the one who skips meetings, and talks to her boyfriend every minute of the day."

"Well, I'm not the one who gets jealous because of a haircut and some clothes — "

"Jealous? Me, jealous of you? Dream on, Mary Anne!"

Dawn stomped down to the bottom of the stairs.

"Wait!" I said.

Dawn turned around. "I don't have time to listen to you. *I* didn't have the whole evening to lounge around the house and admire my boy haircut and clown makeup!"

"Oh, go choke on an alfalfa sprout."

Dawn stormed out of sight. I ran into my room and slammed the door. I was *furious*! Boy haircut? Clown makeup? How *dare* she? That was what I got for trying to talk things out with . . . a witch! I should never have even bothered.

I plopped on my bed and buried my face in the pillow. I was *never* going to talk to Dawn again. I wished I'd never met her. I wished my dad and her mom had hated each other in high school, so they hadn't gotten married. I wished . . .

In the middle of my third wish, my mind turned to soup. I started to cry like a baby. I cried so hard, my sobs came in big hiccups.

But I kept my face in the pillow. I was *not* going to let Dawn hear that I was upset.

Well, you know how it is with a big cry. Sometimes it just puts things in perspective. When I sat up, my pillowcase was soggy but my head was clearer.

And all I could think was, Mary Anne, you really blew it.

Dawn had been mean, and her comments still stung. But I hadn't exactly been full of compassion myself.

I took a deep breath and decided to try again. Dabbing my face with a tissue, I opened my door and went downstairs.

Dawn was in the kitchen, sulking over a pot of boiling tofu. Outside I could hear Dad pulling into the driveway and Sharon greeting him. Dawn didn't look up when I came in.

"Hi," I said.

Dawn grunted.

"Smells good," I said. Okay, I lied.

"Mm-hm," Dawn said.

"Um, I'm sorry."

"Yeah. Right." *I'm sorry, too, Mary Anne* was what I was sort of hoping to hear. But I guess I had to take what I could get.

"Um, I really do want to talk," I said. "Nicely, if possible. No throwing tofu allowed."

I saw a teeny smile on Dawn's lips. That

was a good sign. "Should we have a referee?" she asked.

This time we both smiled. Then we quickly looked at the floor.

A car door slammed outside. "Let's go upstairs," I suggested.

"Okay."

When we reached my room, I sat on the bed and Dawn sat on the desk chair. I looked at the pattern on the bedspread. Dawn looked at the interesting weave of the rug.

I hated the silence. "Um, anyway," I finally said, "I'm sorry . . ."

"You said that already."

"Well, you said some pretty mean things, too," I pointed out, trying not to sound too harsh.

"Mean? Look who's talking about mean!"

"I didn't do anything to hurt you!"

Dawn's mouth dropped open in disbelief. "No? Maybe you forgot about that trip to the mall two weeks ago."

"All I did was get a haircut and buy some nice stuff. What was the big deal?"

"Mary Anne, we're sisters, remember? We always used to talk to each other about everything. All our problems, all the big changes we were going through. . . . You didn't even tell me you were going to get your hair cut."

"*Daawwwn* — "

"It's not as stupid as it sounds, Mary Anne. What if I was thinking about dyeing my hair, or eating a steak dinner — something I'd never done before? Wouldn't you feel left out if I didn't ask your advice or tell you about it or include you in any way? I mean, you went from L. L. Bean to cover girl overnight! I'd have loved picking out clothes with you — even just being excited with you. Instead, you went shopping with your dad."

"Well, the trip was his suggestion," I protested. "You know, a father-daughter thing. I couldn't help that."

Dawn sighed. "I know. I guess that was part of it, too. You two looked so happy and close that day, and I felt left out. It was like he and you were doing something behind my back. And the feeling got worse when you started spending so much time with Logan. *All* the girls felt that, not just me."

"Okay," I said. "I can see how you might have felt about the makeover and the mall trip, Dawn. But I wasn't trying to hurt you. I just wanted to surprise you. I thought you'd be happy. I thought everyone would. I mean, you and Kristy and Claudia and Stacey — you're always telling me to stand up for myself and be independent. Then, when I finally do something independent, you treat me like a traitor. And I was spending all that time with Logan because he was the only person who was nice to me."

"But then you went behind his back with that other guy — "

"Carlos!" I laughed. "Wow, if I ever meet this guy, I'm going to tell him what a mess he's made of my life!"

"What?"

I shook my head. "It's just a dumb rumor. I wouldn't know Carlos if I passed him on the street."

"You mean, Sabrina . . . ?"

"Well, *somebody* started it."

"Wow. I guess we were all assuming a lot of things."

"Yeah," I agreed. "A lot."

We both caught our breath. There was so much to think about.

"I'm sorry, Mary Anne," Dawn said softly. "I think it was hard for me to see you change."

"We all change," I answered, shrugging. "But that doesn't mean we can't like each other. Can't we be friends even if I have short hair?"

There it was. Dawn's fabulous smile. "Okay," she said.

We threw our arms around each other. Dawn burst out laughing.

As for me, what do you think I did?

At least I didn't douse my pillowcase again.

Well, Rounds One and Two were over. Logan trusted me again, and Dawn had finally stopped being so nasty.

Round Three took place on Wednesday at five-thirty.

Yes, I went to the Baby-sitters Club meeting that afternoon. (And let me tell you, that record book was a *disgrace* — but that's another story.)

When I entered Claudia's room with Dawn, the room went completely silent, just as I had expected. Only Jessi and Mal (who had been innocent bystanders during this ordeal) smiled at me, and I could tell they felt self-conscious about it.

Well, I won't bore you with the details of our long, *long* discussion. It was a lot like the one Dawn and I had had, only with many more voices and the smell of Goobers in the air. (Oh, also a few phone interruptions.)

By the end of it everyone was laughing, except me. I hadn't realized how much I'd missed my friends. I felt so happy to be with them I couldn't stop from crying again.

And you know what else? All of them —

everyone — told me how great my hair looked.

After all that!

When we had settled into our comfortable positions, and I was letting a Goober melt in my mouth, I remembered something important.

"Oh, boy," I said. "Tomorrow is supposed to be Carolyn's first flight. All those kids are going to show up. We have to do something." I told my friends what was going to happen at the Arnolds' house.

"Those kids are going to be so disappointed," Stacey said.

"Disappointed?" Claudia repeated. "If Carolyn doesn't give them their money back, they'll tear the basement apart."

"It's my fault," I said. "I shouldn't have let it get out of hand. I just didn't know what to do."

"You could have called one of us," Stacey said.

I nodded. "Yeah. I know."

"I think I'm sitting there tomorrow," Kristy said.

I opened up the record book. My stomach turned at the horrible, sloppy mess of pen smudges and loose papers inside! "Yuck," I said under my breath. I looked under Thursday and saw this:

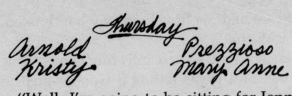

Thursday

Arnold   Prezzioso
Kristy   Mary Anne

"Well, I'm going to be sitting for Jenny and Andrea," I said. "Maybe I should bring them over, so I can help you out. I think you'll need it when the kids come."

Kristy raised her eyebrows. "Uh, yeah. And bring a helmet."

CHAPTER 14

"Is it going to be scary?" Jenny Prezzioso whined for the five-hundredth time. "I hate scary things."

"No," I said, pushing open the Arnolds' door. "And don't forget, I'll be with you the whole time. You'll be safe."

"Andrea will, too?"

"Andrea will, too."

"Geeeeeeaaaaaa," was Andrea's contribution to the discussion.

Jenny is four, and quite . . . well, *spoiled*. It took me a long time to convince her to go to the Arnolds'. (Andrea was much easier. She's only a baby.)

"Are you guys coming or what?" Marilyn shouted from the basement as we walked in.

"Yes!" I called back.

I took Andrea out of her stroller. Holding her in one arm and taking Jenny's hand, I descended with them both into the Realm of Warps and Wormholes.

"Everything is *red*!" Jenny exclaimed, shaking. The basement was dead silent. Even I was a little spooked out.

"That's because Carolyn switched light bulbs," I whispered, pointing to a red bulb.

"Welcome, fellow travelers!" Carolyn said, rushing to meet us at the bottom of the stairs. In the red light, with her goggles and earmuffs, plus a set of springy antennae, she looked like a refugee from the planet Pluto.

"Waaaaaaaahhhhhh!" Andrea wailed.

I buried her face in my shoulder. "Shhh . . . it's all right . . ."

Fortunately Jenny was fascinated. "Is that you, Carolyn?"

"Dr. Arnold to you, young lady!" Carolyn said. "The brilliant Dr. Arnold!"

Jenny laughed. "Doctor? Are you going to give me a shot?"

Ignoring her, Carolyn said, "Follow me."

She led us to the back of the basement, which was hidden by a huge blanket suspended on a rope. Behind the blanket were four folding chairs. Kristy and Marilyn were sitting on two of them, grinning.

Against the wall, the time machine (and the boiler) were covered with taped-together sheets. Jenny and I took our seats and waited for the show to begin.

"This is a special day," Carolyn announced. "I shall demonstrate my time machine to you alone, before the masses arrive." She reached out and grabbed the sheet. "And now, the moment we have all been waiting for! Ladies and gentlemen — "

Jenny giggled again. "Silly, there are just *girls* here!"

" — and children of all ages!" Carolyn barged on. "The time machine!"

She pulled off the sheet.

Jenny gasped. I almost did, too. The machine looked much different now. Carolyn had put tinfoil over the sides of the cartons, and all kinds of dials, bells, gauges, gears, and antennae had been attached. A huge lever stuck out of the side, made from a broom handle. Everything was connected with wires to a real generator on the floor (at least that was what it looked like).

The cartons actually formed four walls with an opening. There was just enough room for a chair inside. A curtain was draped across the front (something like those instant photo booths at amusement parks).

I almost jumped out of my seat when Carolyn reached inside to press a button and I heard these zapping and bubbling noises.

"It's a tape recorder," Marilyn said. "She got the tape at a — "

"Silence!" Carolyn commanded. "Now, Miss Arnold, are you prepared to travel to your requested time — Paris, France, in the year nineteen hundred?"

"Yeah!" Marilyn said. "Ooh, I can't wait! 'Bye, everybody!"

She ran into the machine and plopped onto the seat. "Are you sure you can get me back in time for dinner, Carolyn?"

"Uh, yes!"

"And I don't need any, like, special money, or warm clothing, or anything?"

Carolyn was beginning to look uncomfortable. "I don't think so . . ."

"All right. Well, this better be worth that dollar I paid you." Marilyn pulled the curtain closed. "And I'll be really mad if you don't get me back!"

Now Jenny looked frightened. "Is she really going away?" she asked.

"Just for a little while!" Marilyn called from behind the curtain.

Carolyn's eyes were darting all around. Her fingers seemed frozen around the broom handle. I recognized the look on her face. I had seen it on another of our charges, Charlotte Johannsen, when she had to recite a poem in front of an audience.

Carolyn had stage fright. And I thought I knew why.

I leaned over to Kristy. "Can you take Andrea for a minute?"

Fortunately Andrea was on the way to a nap. She fussed as I took her off my shoulder, then nuzzled happily on Kristy's.

"Excuse me," I said aloud. "This is an emergency high-tech consultation about the, um, flux capacitator."

"Hurry it up," Marilyn said.

I took Carolyn into the corner and knelt down. "Are you okay?" I asked.

"Uh-huh."

"A little nervous after spending all that time building the machine?"

She nodded meekly.

"Carolyn, what do you *really* think will happen when you pull that lever?" I asked.

Carolyn squirmed. I could see the brilliant Dr. Arnold trying to break through. Finally her face fell and she sighed. "Nothing."

I remembered when I was eight and I was convinced I was a fairy princess. I kind of figured if I *said* I was, then I was! I was sure I'd convinced some of my friends, too — until finally they asked me to wave my wand and fly onto the roof of the house. When I didn't, they laughed at me. I ran inside and cried the rest of the night. I threw away my costume, and I never had that fantasy again.

I could see something like that happening to Carolyn.

"Don't look so sad," I said to her. "You built something really amazing. Everyone will enjoy going in it."

"But — but I thought maybe it would work," she said. "I mean, there *could* be a real time machine someday."

"Sure. But meanwhile you can still have fun with *your* machine. Remember all those time travel books you told Jessi you read? Those are pretend adventures. You knew it, but it didn't matter that the stories didn't really, truly happen, right? You still loved reading them."

Carolyn grinned. "Yeah! We can *pretend* to take trips to other times and places!" Her eyes were darting back to that lever again.

"There's just one thing, Carolyn," I went on. "When the kids come later on, maybe you should offer to give them back their money."

"Okay," Carolyn said, nodding solemnly. She pulled a dollar out of her pocket and stuck it through the curtain to Marilyn. "Here."

"What's this for?" Marilyn asked.

"To buy yourself a hot dog in . . . Paris in nineteen hundred!" With a dramatic flourish, she pulled down the lever. A bell rang and some gears turned. We oohed and aahed.

Then, turning her back, Carolyn made eerie screeching noises and announced, "The years roll back . . . nineteen fifty, forty, twenty, zero! You're in Paris, the Feivel Tower!"

"Eiffel!" Marilyn called.

Carolyn turned to face us. Her antennae wobbled back and forth. "Now, ladies and gentlemen, our traveler is in the wormhole of the space/time continual, light-years away — "

"Wormhole?" Jenny said. "Ew!"

"Now comes the most difficult part," Carolyn went on. "To bring her back, we must position the flux capacitator at exactly the spot of electronic, uh, flux." She turned her back and screamed, "Weeeee-oooooo, weeee-ooooo! Now you're coming back! Poof!" She paused solemnly by the curtain, then yanked it open. "And there she is! Living proof, ladies and gentlemen!"

"Yeeeaa!" We clapped and cheered and stamped our feet. Andrea whimpered, then went back to sleep.

And Marilyn stood up, wide-eyed and ecstatic, like Dorothy seeing the Emerald City for the first time. "It was amazing! I had this big frilly dress, and the organ grinder's monkey danced for me, and I saw this incredible ballet dancer named Mickinsky . . ."

As she went on and on, I could see the happiness playing across Carolyn's face

— even underneath the goggles.

"Can I go next?" Jenny whispered, tugging on my sleeve.

Somehow, I knew things were going to work out just fine.

For the rest of the afternoon, kids filed into the basement. Carolyn became more and more confident about her "trips." A couple of the kids felt cheated, but most enjoyed the game. And they *all* got their money back. Kristy and I made sure of that.

Afterward, Kristy and I walked to my house (I'd invited her for dinner). It felt wonderful to be friends again.

"You know, the way you handled Carolyn was incredible," Kristy said.

"Well, I knew how she felt. When I had trouble figuring out what was real and what was fantasy, I don't remember anyone talking to me about it. So I wanted to make sure I did with Carolyn."

Kristy exhaled and watched a frosty white cloud circle her face and disappear. "Yeah. I guess it's important to talk when things get confusing, huh?"

I gave my friend a big smile. "I guess."

"Oh, by the way . . . " Kristy said.

"What?"

"I really do like your haircut."

CHAPTER 15

"Do you have Honey Rose?" I said breathlessly, running into Dawn's room.

Dawn turned around on her dressing table seat. There was an hour to go before we were leaving for the January Jamboree, and I had run out of blush. "Um, I doubt it. That's not my color." She rummaged through a drawer full of makeup. "How about Peaches and Cream?" she said, flipping open a compact.

"No," I said. "Too pinkish."

She held up another. "Nantucket Sand?"

"Too dark."

I reached in and pulled the top off an old pancake container that said Spring Blossom. "This looks about right," I said.

"Great. You can use my sponge. I'm using a brush."

I took the sponge, then dabbed a little of the blush on my cheek.

The color was a tiny bit lighter than Honey

Rose. "Well, I just hope I don't look like a ghost."

"Don't worry."

I ran into my room and finished my makeup, then put on the dress I had bought at Steven E. My hair got messed up, so I brushed it out. Then I ran back into Dawn's room. "Can you zip me up?"

Dawn turned to me with this huge smile. "You look *stunning!*"

"I do?"

"Wow!"

For the first time I noticed Dawn's dress. It was made of black velvet, with a sheer bodice trimmed with beading and lace, and a flared, above-knee skirt. With black stockings and shoes, and her hair pulled up in a French braid, Dawn looked absolutely breathtaking. "You should talk!" I said. "Pete Black is going to faint when he sees you!"

Pete, the eighth-grade president, was Dawn's date that night. It was the first time they had ever gone out.

"Thanks!" Dawn said. "Now hold still."

She pulled the zipper up the back of my dress and fastened the hook on top. I spun around and looked at myself in Dawn's mirror. "Oooooh, watch out, *Logan!*" I said, shimmying a little.

Dawn burst out laughing.

"What's so funny?" I said.

"I can't get over how much you have changed, Mary Anne!"

I could feel myself turning red. "I was just kidding around."

"It's okay. You're allowed. It's cute."

"You see? You've changed, too!" I said. "It really bothered you when I first stopped being this demure, plain stepsister."

Dawn nodded. "Yeah." She sat down again. I could tell the unpleasant memories were racing through her head. She sighed. "You know, Mary Anne, I was just thinking."

I sat down next to her. "What?"

"Well, seeing you so close to your dad really affected me."

"I know. You said that."

"Yeah, but I didn't tell you why it bothered me so much. It was just that . . . well, it made me think of my dad. Mary Anne, I miss him so much sometimes. I mean, your dad's great to me, but *you're* his daughter. And it was hard to see that."

"I kind of figured that out, Dawn," I said gently.

"Well, I just wanted to tell you myself. And I realize it was unfair of me to put that on you. I guess it's something I have to work out."

I smiled and put my arm around her. "Well, it helps to talk about it," I said. "And you're forgiven."

I don't think I will ever forget the January Jamboree. The SMS gym glittered. Hundreds of foil snowflakes hung from the ceiling, lit by spinning lights. An art class had painted a gorgeous winter mural, showing a turn-of-the-century New England winter scene. It stretched from one end of the gym to the other. The chaperones wore gowns and tuxedos, the DJ was fantastic, and the food was delicious. It was elegant, elegant, elegant.

You should have seen Logan in a tuxedo. He looked sensational. I could feel everyone staring at us whenever we danced (it didn't hurt that Logan is an expert dancer).

There were other spectacular sights, too. Like Kristy Thomas trying to walk with heels in a long dress (she kicked them off about two minutes after she got to the gym). And Claudia Kishi, wearing a lamé outfit that was all sharp angles and flashy colors. And Stacey McGill, looking as if she had stepped out of a Hollywood movie in a slinky silk gown that belonged to her mother. Her date was Sam Thomas, Kristy's older brother, who kept grossing people out with a rubber tarantula until Stacey asked him to stop.

But the best part was the dancing. During one of the slow numbers, as Logan spun me around the floor, Dawn and Pete swung by. "You guys are stealing the show!" Dawn said.

"Uh-uh. Not while *you're* on the dance floor," I said.

As we danced away, Logan said, "You know, for awhile I was afraid you and Dawn would never talk to each other again."

"Yeah," I said. "But you know what? We're closer than ever."

Logan smiled that famous make-you-melt smile. "Yes, we are." He blushed as soon as he said that, but I thought it was sweet. I smiled and hugged him tighter.

After the song, Logan and I walked toward the refreshment table with Dawn and Pete. Out of the corner of my eye, I spotted Sabrina entering the gym with her date. She was laughing giddily, in an incredible sequined gown. I made a mental note to say hi later on.

"Hey, whatever happened with Carolyn's time machine?" Logan asked, ladling us some punch.

I told him about the afternoon at the Arnolds'. Logan, Dawn, and Pete listened closely and laughed at the funny parts. Then Pete said, "Wouldn't it be great if the machine really worked?"

Everyone nodded in agreement.

"Where would you go if it did?" I asked.

"Super Bowl Three," Pete said. "Nineteen sixty-eight. Joe Namath and the New York Jets. Incredible upset victory."

Dawn pretended to yawn. "Bor-ing."

"I know where I'd go," Logan said.

"Where?" I asked.

"To the day I first saw you. I liked that feeling."

Boy, did I turn red.

"Awwwwwwww . . ." Pete groaned. "Give me a break!"

Logan shrugged. "I can't help it."

"I know where I'd go," Dawn said, looking straight at me with a glint in her eye. "I'd go back to this room, about twenty-three years ago, to see my mom and your dad at one of *their* school dances."

"Yeah!" I agreed.

"Complete with horses and carriages," Logan remarked.

"Ooh, listen!" Dawn said as a great rock tune came on. "This is one of my favorites! Let's dance!"

The four of us moved onto the dance floor. For the second time, I caught a glimpse of Sabrina and her date. Sabrina looked about twenty years old and so did her date. He was very tall, with thick black hair and dark, handsome features.

Dawn noticed them, too. "Who's the guy?" she asked, dancing close to Logan and me.

"I don't know," I said.

Suddenly Logan, Dawn, and I all stopped dancing at once. We turned to each other with identical wide-eyed expressions on our faces. Pete stared at us as if we'd lost our minds.

"Carlos!" we said in unison.

At the other end of the room, Sabrina's date looked around. Then he smiled, shrugged his shoulders, and continued dancing.

Off in our corner, I thought we'd never stop laughing.

About the Author

ANN M. MARTIN did *a lot* of baby-sitting when she was growing up in Princeton, New Jersey. She is a former editor of books for children, and was graduated from Smith College.

Ms. Martin lives in New York City with her cats, Mouse and Rosie. She likes ice cream and *I Love Lucy;* and she hates to cook.

Ann Martin's Apple Paperbacks include *Yours Turly, Shirley; Ten Kids, No Pets; With You and Without You; Bummer Summer;* and all the other books in the Baby-sitters Club series.

Look for #61

JESSI AND THE AWFUL SECRET

As I bit into my fry I realized I was having a good time. These kids were talking to me as if I were as old as they were and their equal in every way. I looked to Mary to see if she was having fun.

All I could read from her expression was nervousness. She'd barely eaten one fry. Instead, she'd broken them in half and was moving them around on her tray. If you weren't paying attention, it looked as if she'd eaten more than she actually had. Occasionally, she sipped on her soda, but the level hadn't gone down much.

I came up with several reasons why she wasn't eating. One was nerves. Or maybe she didn't want to spoil her dinner. It could have been that she truly hated fast food. (Dawn would consider eating this kind of food inhuman torture.) There might have been a lot of reasons why, but I sure hope it wasn't because she was on a diet.

The diet reason worried me. And here was another puzzling question. Why didn't she just say she wasn't going to eat? No one would have cared. Why try to hide the fact that she wasn't eating?

Before I could worry about it much more, my father walked into the Burger King. " 'Bye, everyone," I said, quickly gathering my coat and dance bag.

Everyone waved. "So long, Jess," said Darcy.

"See you again Tuesday," added Raul.

"Those kids are a bit older than you, aren't they?" said my father as we got into the car. (He is *so* overprotective!)

"Yeah, but they're real nice," I told him. It was true. All of them were nice. Even Vince was okay. And I was especially getting to like Mary. I admired the way she disagreed with Raul even though she had a crush on him. I'd also noticed she had a pleasant way with the kids. Mary was turning out to be real nice, all right. But I was concerned about the food thing. I just hoped she was okay.

**Read all the latest books
in the Baby-sitters Club series
by Ann M. Martin**

#10 *Logan Likes Mary Anne!*
Mary Anne has a crush on a *boy* baby-sitter!

#11 *Kristy and the Snobs*
The kids in Kristy's new neighborhood are
S-N-O-B-S!

#12 *Claudia and the New Girl*
Claudia might give up the club — and it's all Ash-
ley's fault!

#13 *Good-bye Stacey, Good-bye*
Oh no! Stacey McGill is moving back to New York!

#14 *Hello, Mallory*
Is Mallory Pike good enough to join the club?

#15 *Little Miss Stoneybrook . . . and Dawn*
Everyone in Stoneybrook has gone beauty-
pageant crazy!

#16 *Jessi's Secret Language*
Jessi's new charge is teaching her a *secret language*.

#17 *Mary Anne's Bad-Luck Mystery*
Will Mary Anne's bad luck ever go away?

#18 *Stacey's Mistake*
Has Stacey made a big mistake by inviting the
Baby-sitters to New York City?

#19 *Claudia and the Bad Joke*
Claudia is headed for trouble when she baby-sits
for a practical joker.

THE BABY-SITTERS Club®

by Ann M. Martin

More titles... ▶

The Baby-sitters Club titles continued...

Available wherever you buy books...or use this order form.

Scholastic Inc., P.O. Box 7502, 2931 E. McCarty Street, Jefferson City, MO 65102

Please send me the books I have checked above. I am enclosing $_____
(please add $2.00 to cover shipping and handling). Send check or money order - no
cash or C.O.D.s please.

Name _____

Address _____

City_____ State/Zip_____

Tell us your birth date! _____

© 1992 Walt Disney Company.

It's a Super Special Month!

YOU CAN WIN A TRIP TO WALT DISNEY WORLD RESORT®!

Enter The Winter Super Special Giveaway for The Baby-sitters Club® and Baby-sitters Little Sister® fans!

Visit Walt Disney World Resort...and experience all the excitement of Peter Pan, Tinkerbell, and a whole cast of characters! We'll send the **Grand Prize Winner** of this Giveaway and his/her parent or guardian (age 21 or older) on an all-expense paid trip, for 5 days and 4 nights, to Walt Disney World Resort in Florida!

10 Second Prize Winners get a Baby-sitters Club Record Album!
25 Third Prize Winners get a Baby-sitters Club T-shirt!

Early Bird Bonus!
100 early entries will receive a Baby-sitters Club calendar! But hurry!
To qualify, your entry must be postmarked by December 1, 1992.

Just fill in the coupon below or write the information on a 3" x 5" piece of paper and mail to:
THE WINTER SUPER SPECIAL GIVEAWAY, P.O. Box 7500, Jefferson City, MO 65102.
Return by March 31, 1993.

Rules: Entries must be postmarked by March 31, 1993. Winners will be picked at random and notified by mail. No purchase necessary. Valid only in the U.S. Void where prohibited. Taxes on prizes are the responsibility of the winners and their immediate families. Employees of Scholastic Inc.; its agencies, affiliates, subsidiaries; and their immediate families are not eligible. For a complete list of winners, send a self-addressed stamped envelope after March 31, 1993 to: The Winter Super Special Giveaway Winners List, at the address provided above.

- -

The Winter Super Special Giveaway

Name_____ Age _____

Street _____

City_____ State/Zip _____

Where did you buy this book?

☐ Bookstore   ☐ Drugstore   ☐ Supermarket   ☐ Library
☐ Book Club   ☐ Book Fair   ☐ Other_____ (specify)   BSC692

Pssst... Know what? You can find out **everything** there is to know about *The Baby-sitters Club*. Join the BABY-SITTERS FAN CLUB! Get the hot news on the series, the inside scoop on all the Baby-sitters, and lots of baby-sitting fun...just for $4.95!

With your **two-year** membership, you get:

★ An official membership card!
★ A colorful banner!
★ The exclusive Baby-sitters Fan Club quarterly newsletter with baby-sitting tips, activities and more!

Just fill in the coupon below and mail with payment to:
THE BABY-SITTERS FAN CLUB,
Scholastic Inc., P.O. Box 7500, 2931 E. McCarty Street, Jefferson City, MO 65012.

The Baby-sitters Fan Club

❏ **YES!** Enroll me in The Baby-sitters Fan Club! I've enclosed my check or money order (no cash please) for $4.95 made payable to Scholastic Inc.

Name _____ Age _____

Street _____

City _____ State/Zip _____

Where did you buy this *Baby-sitters Club* book?

❏ Bookstore   ❏ Drugstore   ❏ Supermarket   ❏ Book Club
❏ Book Fair   ❏ Other_____(specify)
Not available outside of U.S. and Canada.